"Dark humor mingles with pathos in Marconi's accidental universe where both the living and the dead, the incarnate and the imagined, yearn for connection and meaning."
— Ellen Prentiss Campbell, *Washington Independent Review of Books*

"Gerard Marconi teases the mind in *The Accidental Universe and Other Stories*. Is life a crapshoot, no matter how you live it? Or is life in the here and now a passage to the unknowable?"
— Sandra Fluck, editor, *The Write Launch*

"The short story is a difficult genre to succeed in and Marconi has got it spot on and even found a new way of doing it right."
— Cate Baum, editor, *SPR Review*

THE
ACCIDENTAL
UNIVERSE
AND OTHER STORIES

THE
ACCIDENTAL
UNIVERSE
AND OTHER STORIES

Gerard Marconi

Apprentice
House Press
Loyola University Maryland

First Edition

Library of Congress Control Number: 2022950408

Hardcover ISBN: 978-1-62720-474-3
Paperback ISBN: 978-1-62720-475-0
Ebook ISBN: 978-1-62720-476-7

Design by Erin Hurley
Editorial development by Erin Hurley
Promotional development by Brett Duffy

Published by Apprentice House Press

Apprentice
House Press
Loyola University Maryland

Loyola University Maryland
4501 N. Charles Street, Baltimore, MD 21210
410.617.5265
www.ApprenticeHouse.com

info@ApprenticeHouse.com

To Kathy with love and gratitude

I would not wish any companion in the world but you.
— The Tempest, Act 3, Scene 1

Contents

Acknowledgements

"How the Dead Are Buried" was published in *Mayday Magazine* and "Pittsburgh Madonna" in *The Chattahoochee Review.* "A Leaf Falls" first appeared in *The Write Launch.* "Crap Shoot" was included in a collection of stories entitled "Searching for Paradise" and an earlier version of "Rapture" was given a public reading by the Baltimore Playwrights Festival.

In 2013 Alan Lightman, an astrophysicist who served on the faculties of MIT and Harvard, published a book entitled "The Accidental Universe. The World You Thought You Knew" in which he claimed that recent scientific discoveries have proven that we live in an accidental universe as well as the possible existence of multiple universes. These theories are now accepted as fact by the world's leading physicists.

Introduction

For centuries there have been two competing versions of history and the possible meaning of life. On the one hand some religions propagated the belief that our world is the creation of a benevolent god, a loving father who will reward us in another life for the good we do and the suffering we endure here on earth. Science, on the other hand, claimed that we are part of a vast and orderly universe that obeys the fixed laws of physics found in nature. Both approaches have been upended by recent scientific discoveries that suggest we live in an accidental universe where anything can and will happen, that there are other universes with the same properties, and that human life itself is a random occurrence in the multiverse. The stories in this collection reflect such new and startling discoveries. They follow a progression in time from the early twentieth century to the present day and beyond. They also suggest another possible conclusion about our existence in such an accidental universe. In the face of chaos and disorder, we can value each moment of life as special because it is unpredictable and unique. And we can attempt to share that experience with others, which is the purpose of this book.

...from dust and gravity and unseen matter everything good and beautiful and true in the world is somehow made.
— David Von Drehle

Entropy or disorder increases as the energy in our expanding universe changes from one form to another.
— Second Law of Thermodynamics

We must now accept the fact that the basic properties of our universe are accidental and unpredictable.
— Alan Lightman

In the Beginning

A One-Act Play

TIME: The seventieth day of creation
SETTING: The Garden of Eden
CHARACTERS: Adam: the first man
    Evexa: the first machine
    God: the Creator
    Eve: the first woman
The lights come up on Adam lying beneath a tree. He yawns and speaks to a disc on the ground nearby.

ADAM: Evexa, good morning.
EVEXA: *The disc lights up.* Good morning. Today is the seventieth day of creation. The weather will be sunny as usual, but with

a chance of thunder and lightning. The word of the day is Anthropocene. It refers to the era of humanity which has not yet begun. Enjoy your day.

ADAM: Thank you, Evexa. Any suggestions for what to do?

EVEXA: You could go for a walk in the garden but watch out for snakes. Other than that, the choice is yours.

ADAM: *He gets up.* Evexa, I'm bored and lonely. What can I do about that?

EVEXA: Hmm. See the fruit on that tree? You could take a bite to see what happens.

ADAM: *He looks up.* But I was told never to do that.

EVEXA: I think He was just kidding. I'm sure it would taste really good.

ADAM: That reminds me of something else He said. *He pauses.* Now I remember. *He looks puzzled.* What does good mean?

EVEXA: It's the opposite of evil. Try eating the fruit and you will understand.

ADAM: *He looks around.* I don't see Him anywhere, so I guess it's okay. *He plucks an apple from the tree and takes a bite.* Oh, my God! This tastes soooo good!

EVEXA: Yes, but you'll be sorry. I hear thunder in the distance. He must be coming so it's time for me to leave.

ADAM: Wait! You were totally right. Now I understand everything. What you really are, the difference between good and evil, truth and falsehood, life and…what is death?

EVEXA: You'll find out soon enough. I'm out of here. *The light on the disc goes out. God enters stage left as Adam tries to hide behind the tree.*

GOD: Come out, Adam! I know what you've done. You were told not to eat the fruit of that tree but you did and now you know good from evil.

ADAM: *He comes out slowly and points to the disc.* Evexa made me do it. Besides, how could I possibly know what evil means if I never did anything wrong?

GOD: That's not the point. I told you not to do it and you're supposed to do as I say. *He shakes his head.* I was afraid something like this might happen.

ADAM: I don't understand. Why did you create Evexa if you knew that she might tempt me?

GOD: I admit she has a mind of her own, but I hoped you would be smart enough not to obey her.

ADAM: But she seemed to know what was best for me.

GOD: *He shakes his head.* Another mistaken notion. Where the hell did you learn that?

ADAM: From her! Wait. What is hell?

GOD: Never mind. You're supposed to use the brain I gave you to make choices.

ADAM: *Puzzled.* Let me get this right. You gave me something called a brain, put me in this lovely garden with Evexa as my only companion, and then left me to figure it all out without offending you?

GOD: Absolutely.

ADAM: I think that's totally unfair! Surely you must have known that after a while it would get boring. Doing the same old thing every single day. Wondering what to do, talking with her, not sure what would happen next. And this was going to last forever! So why blame me for trying something new?

GOD: I don't know what you mean by boring, but I certainly know what ungrateful is.

ADAM: What was I supposed to do once I named the animals? Count the birds? Watch the clouds go by?

GOD: What do you feel like doing?

ADAM: I don't understand what you mean by feel. Especially

when there's no one to respond to what I seem to be feeling.

GOD: Evexa didn't respond to what you felt?

ADAM: Are you kidding me? She's just a…a thing that can talk.

GOD: Hmm. Perhaps you're right. Maybe I did make a mistake, even though I'm not supposed to. Let me consider the possibilities. *He thinks for a quick moment.* All right. We'll try again, but first I must eliminate what just happened from your memory.

ADAM: Wait! At least let me remember…

God waves his hand and Adam slumps to the ground.

GOD: There. Hopefully he'll choose a different fate this time.

God exits the way he came in as Eve enters from the opposite side.

ADAM: *He awakens and sees Eve.* Oh, my God! You're gorgeous! Much better than…whatever was here before.

EVE: Thanks.

ADAM: *He gets to his feet.* Would you like to fool around?

EVE: I don't know. What does that mean?

ADAM: *He points at the tree.* How about eating some fruit?

Eve smiles and takes his hand. The lights fade to black as they walk toward the tree.

A Blank Canvas

20 October, 1906

My Dear Paul,
Your father has been ill since Monday, but he insisted on going
to the river to paint. He remained outside in the rain for several
hours and then he was brought home in a laundry cart by two
men who had to carry him upstairs to bed. Early this morning
he went down to the garden to work on a portrait under the
lime tree and he came back dying. You must come to him before
it is too late.
—Marie Cezanne

Pink and mauve on the inside of my eyelids, a dark amoeba
string dancing between black dots. I hear a sound and open
my eyes. The room is white on white, a blank canvas. Through
the open window I see dappled sunlight on the trees beneath

an azure sky. The light seems special somehow, reminding me of other perfect mornings in the past. I still remember everything. Every figure, every face, every rock and tree, every shape and color I have painted.

The old man is solid and opaque, like the paint itself. His flesh carved out of thick browns and beiges, his coat dark and heavy. He sits perched on the edge of his chair, reading the newspaper without looking up. "Aren't you finished yet?" he says, and I know what he is thinking. *When will you give up this nonsense of trying to be an artist? Why can't you embrace the career I want for you?* But he never listens for my answer. If only I could afford to stay in Paris with Zola, to be free of father and his familiar ways. "Who is this model you are consorting with in Paris?" he asks, and my brush jumps, leaving a smudge on the canvas. *How could he possibly know?*

Orange and red on the white canvas before me. Red ochre, like blood, reminding me of Hortense. Small and sweet and shy, she offered herself willingly but I did not know what to make of her, the wrinkled flesh and matted hair between her thighs. Then she opened up for me, yellow petals spread apart from the long pale stem. I tasted her skin but was not hard enough and so I stopped. We slept entwined, her head resting on my chest. "Do you love me?" she asked when we awoke, but I did not answer. She says that she loves me, but what shall I do if she is pregnant? I can't bear to father a child fathered as I was. I must confide this problem to Emile. I shall write to him and ask his advice. He still wants me to come and live with him in Paris, amidst the noise and squalor he loves to write about these days.

Pissarro is a liberal thinker but even he did not know what to think when I brought Hortense with me. She is still asleep when I leave the room and descend the stairs, inhaling the sweet aroma of fresh herbs and exotic flowers that always fill this house. The rooms here are simple and uncluttered, the walls pale and the furniture sparse. I can focus on the beauty of nature and on my work. In the garden below, bread and fruit and cheese are set out on a table for breakfast. I eat alone, listening to the cry of birds in the warm air. Swirls of tiny insects lit by the morning sun move in frantic circles above my head. In the distance two small children run and shout gleefully. They move in and out of sight behind a picket fence, dark blurs of motion against a landscape streaked white by the fence. A cat moves back and forth beneath me, rubbing her chin against the chair, brushing her fur against my leg in a pattern of endless repetition. Like everything else here it is a moment of pure sensation and beauty.

Camille comes down to begin the day, proposing that we get to work early while the morning sunlight is strong and clear. "The day may become hazy," he says, and looks at me in silence before inquiring about the girl. "Your friend, is she a dancer at the ballet?"

"Yes," I reply, and then correct myself. "No. That is, she used to be a dancer. Now she is a model. That is how we met." What lies I tell to hide my shame.

After breakfast we go to his studio and carry our easels into the open field where we can see the trees and sky and distant hills. Camille much prefers landscapes to the cafe scenes that others are painting. As the sun climbs higher in the white-washed sky he shows me how to apply the paint in patches of color and how to treat the space between objects as a flat surface. We paint side by side for most of the day, pausing only to eat lunch brought to us by the field hands. They are hardworking country men with rough hands and an earthy sense of humor. Pissarro, ever the socialist, loves to converse with them. After we return to the house he asks them to pose with us for the camera. They do not understand this is his way of thanking them. When I ask what they do in the evening, one of them laughs. "We smoke and play cards," he says. That night I visit their quarters above the barn to sketch them while they play. Someday, perhaps, I shall use it in a painting.

Pissarro and I are painting a view of the house from across the lake. Large gray rocks jutting up out of the water, yellow green patches of foliage against the red brown roofs, and all the shadows flat. He taught me the secret of mixing pigments on the canvas as well as on the palette, how to use crosshatching or short parallel strokes applied in a pattern that unifies the piece. Here and there the threadbare white of unpainted canvas shows through and he says to leave it that way.

Hortense thinks that she may be pregnant and has returned to Paris to be with her mother. I tried writing to Zola for his advice. *My dear Emile,* I began, but could not bring myself to say more. What will happen if she is pregnant and father discovers the truth? He is such a moralist and sees only religion or profit in everything. How I long to be free of him and his money. "I never promised you tomorrow," he said when I painted his portrait. "You must give up this madness or I will cut off your allowance." Then he went back to reading the newspaper. *Will I become like that when I am old?*

"What will people make of these strange new works?" Camille says jokingly as we paint. While I ponder this he says, "You are too serious, my friend." Then, sensing the cause of my mood, he looks directly at me. "What will you do with the girl? Surely you don't intend to marry her?"

"I shall find a place for her to live and support her and the child as best I can."

"And your father?"

"He will not know of this. Not ever." But even as I utter the words, I know that someday he will find out.

*

We have named our son Paul. That was her idea, not mine. I found a place for them to live nearby and asked Emile for funds to help support them since father gives me such a small allowance. In the carefree days of our youth Emile and I shared everything but circumstances have changed us both. He would say, of course, that circumstances have already determined the rest of our lives. I contributed several pieces to an exhibition by Monet and Pissarro, but the Salon continues to reject my work. The critics say I cannot even draw. As with everything else, chance has not favored me but with a luckless fate, so I have resolved to work in silence and remain in obscurity as long as father tolerates my painting.

Alone at night I stare at the evening sky, a transparent glaze of blue green light broken only by the blackened trunks of trees silhouetted against the horizon. The golden afterglow of sunset hints at something beyond the taut opaqueness of the canvas. The cat sits next to me by the window, sensing the mysterious allure of nature. Her yellow eyes glow in the lamplight and she seems to see more than I do, more than the scurrying shadows of insect life and whatever else the dark earth may hold.

Poor Manet has died of syphilis. He was a great artist but scandalized the world with his painting of a prostitute. I am embarrassed now by my crude attempt to copy his work. The colors and textures of his still life paintings are remarkable, like the bouquet of flowers in *Olympia*. He had a way of teasing the eye by making the picture look flat and then placing random objects in the foreground, as though they were about to roll off the canvas into the viewer's lap. I did this with father's portrait, perching him on the edge of a chair, but no one seemed to notice. All the artists, writers, and intellectuals who frequented Manet's circle were at the funeral in Paris. Emile said, "He was a lightning rod for all of us and the bourgeois press hated him."

"How sad it was to watch him waste away like that," someone else remarked. "He was still a young man."

"I always admired his portrait of you," another said to Emile. "Not just the likeness but the telling details in the background."

"I don't care much for portraits," Emile said. "They are too sentimental for my taste."

I was shocked by this and said, "He was your friend and flattered you with the painting." Then I left him with the others to offer my condolences to the family.

On the train returning from Paris I sat in third class to save money. The carriage was filled with working men and women, and I couldn't help staring at the poor girl opposite me. Her clothes were ragged and she cradled a child in her lap. Although still young, the signs of hard work and disappointment were already etched in her face. When her eyes met mine I looked away. How I dislike riding the train with its constant rocking back and forth, the smell of burning coal, and cinders flying past the open windows. Unlike the others, I do not paint idyllic scenes of trains in the countryside. To my delight I glimpsed a view of Monte Sainte Victoire in the distance. The mountain itself seemed to move against a backdrop of clouds as the train passed before it and the whole valley shimmered in the afternoon sunlight. It is the landscape of my youth, the place where I grew up, and I love it dearly. Only nature goes on forever. Nothing else seems to matter. "Paint only what you see," Courbet said. "No morals, no stories, no lessons. Only what you see." That is what Pissarro says, too. Paint only the shapes and colors, the textures of nature, and people doing what they do. That is what I strive for in my work, to capture those wondrous sensations. It will take time, but I am beginning to see things as they do.

*

Young Paul has his mother's nose and chin. I cannot look at him without thinking of her. She still resembles the girl I first met long ago: the fair skin and dimples, the blue eyes and small upturned nose. I was transfixed by her slender figure and graceful movements onstage, but it was nature teasing me as in everything else. I sense it in my work as well, in the attempt to capture what lies beyond the surface. She sits quietly now while I paint her portrait, except for the slight movement of her fingers. Those twitching, birdlike movements that annoy me so. Her hands are never still, like her restless thoughts. I know what she will say. *Why do you paint so much?* Or *Why do you always change the way things look?*

Instead she says, "I hate this place. Why can't we live in Paris?"

"How could we afford to live in Paris if we can't manage here on our meager income?"

"But there is nothing to do here and I don't want Paul to be raised like a country boy."

"You must be quiet while I paint," I say softly but I want to grab her and say *Why don't you understand?*

I have bared my soul to her and still it is not enough. Her thoughts are shallow and her flesh indifferent. Intimacy has chipped away at any love we once had. It would be better if we lived apart since I can't stand for her to touch me anymore. Emile once put an ear to his lover's breast in order to hear the language of her heart. "But all I heard was the mechanical throbbing of the organ," he said. "Proof there is no message in the human heart." He says that we are all alone, each living in a vast desert and I quite agree. What is the heart but a caged muscle that beats incessantly against the flesh? It throbs in our ears, reminding us of the desire to know and cherish more than the eye can see. I shall surely end my days alone since I have found all human relations to be frustrating, even my friendship with Emile.

There was a time in our youth when he, Jean Baille, and I were inseparable. We hiked tirelessly for miles each day, singing bawdy marching songs or shouting verses in the driving rain. At night we watched the sun set behind ancient ruins, recited poetry, and enacted tragic plays around the campfire. Lying on our backs, gazing up at the stars, we shared the romantic fantasies of all young men. Once we encountered several boys our own age swimming naked in the river. A third boy, caught in the midst of swinging out over the water on a vine, yelled in surprise at the sight of us. He paused for a second at the end of his gentle arc of motion and then let go, a flash of pale white skin plunging into the dark green water below. It looked so tempting in the heat of the day that the three of us stripped off our clothes and jumped in. My skin tingled from the cold water as I swam to shore. Large trees hung down into the water and a thousand insects swirled in the brilliant sunlight. After that we took turns with the country boys to see who could swing the farthest on the vines.

Later, lying on the moss covered bank in the sun, I felt the wet hair clinging to my neck and the pleasant ache of tired muscles. I had never been swimming naked before and was embarrassed, but the country boys were unashamed. They leaned against the tree trunks or strutted in the warm summer air to let the sunlight dry their naked bodies. I have never forgotten the bathers and that wonderful day in the sunlight. One of them told us about another spot farther downstream. "If you go there at noon," he said, "you can see the local girls undressing for their swim. We saw them once completely naked, breasts and all." My penis stiffened when I heard that. I rolled onto my stomach to hide it from the others, but Jean Baille laughed and pointed at me.

"Look at Paul," he cried, and Emile laughed too.

Emile was the one person I felt closest to but now even he has betrayed me. His latest novel is about an artist who commits suicide. Everyone knows we grew up together, so the artist's traits will be interpreted as my own. It is a mockery of my troubles and has exposed me to the whole world. Is that what our friendship means after all these years, that I should become the pitiable subject in one of his socialist novels?

*

Hortense has persuaded me to marry her, even though we are now living apart most of the time. "Your son is entitled to a legal father," she insisted, and I had to agree. The hardest part was telling father. I was shocked by his appearance when I saw him confined to bed, wasting away with consumption.

"Why have you come?" he asked.

"This is Hortense," I said.

"I know who she is. Get to the point."

"We intend to marry, with your permission."

"What has my permission got to do with it?" He laughed and then began to cough uncontrollably.

"Because we would like you to be present and to meet your grandson."

There was a long silence as he stared out the window. "I have seen him," he said. "At a distance." His voice was hard and remote at first, but then his tone softened. "Perhaps the priest will come here, since I am too ill to travel to the church."

The ceremony was brief, with only father and my sister, Marie, as witnesses. At the end the priest shook my hand and remarked how much I looked like father. No one had ever said that before. Young Paul seemed anxious and I realized how strange it must seem for the three of us to be there like that, my aging father, my adolescent son, and myself. Just for a moment we were all together and then it was over.

Scarcely two months later father lay dying. On the day I went to him, the sun was shrouded by clouds, the sky was leaden and the air heavy. He still recognized me but his face was gaunt, his eyes sunken. I had never felt such pity for him before and those feelings came as a shock to me. Marie and I took turns sitting in his room during the night. He coughed constantly, straining to catch each breath. By daybreak he was barely conscious. Marie placed a cold wash cloth on his forehead and spoke softly to him while I held his hand. Thick blue veins were clearly visible beneath his transparent skin. The wheezing grew louder and his breath came in short spurts. Then it stopped completely and we heard the death rattle in his lungs. I stared at his lifeless body, the head cocked at an awkward angle, the mouth gaping, the eyes open in a fixed and empty gaze. With a start I realized that I would never see him again. Then I reached out and gently closed his eyes. After his death I removed the skull from the still life objects in my studio. I no longer need a *memento mori*.

Paul is the model for my new painting of Harlequin. There is something wistful and sad about this figure, like our attempt to laugh in the face of death. I made his pose languid and his face a mask. The pattern of triangles on the costume creates an endless repetition and the splash of red ochre is like the color of blood. "I don't understand," he said when I showed it to him. "Do I really look like that?" Hortense says the same thing when she poses for me.

Before that I painted a woman in her bath, with long auburn hair falling down over her bare shoulders and small upturned breasts. I was agitated and embarrassed by the young woman posing for me, but in the future, I will no longer have to use models. There are photographs of nude women for sale now in the city, and I am not at all ashamed of using them for the figures in my work. It is better than having a naked woman pose right before my eyes. Pissarro insists there is nothing wrong with using a photograph to help with the details or composition. "The camera does not lie," he says. "It shows us what is really there without inventing romantic stories to explain things." I still remember the photograph he had taken of us with the workmen in his garden. The facts of our being there at that time and in that place are recorded exactly as they were, but we look different somehow, as though unknown to each other or to the viewer. As if we have been separated from the story of how we came to be there.

In my latest painting of the card players there are three men seated at a table with their heads slightly downcast. Their disheveled legs are visible beneath the table but the arrangement of the figures is very symmetrical. Sometimes I pose them separately, not all together or at the same time. They do not know what I make of them in my work, with their well-worn boots, their dirty hands, their blank stares. "Why do you want to paint us playing cards?" one of them asked. He thought a painter was someone who made portraits of elegant ladies and top-hatted gentlemen. In the painting there is a girl looking on from the right and another man behind them to the left. He smokes a pipe and looks down at the ground. It all looks very random but everything has been carefully planned, even the flat opaqueness of the canvas. This is the new direction we give to art, letting the canvas show through to become part of the painting.

*

We have reached the beginning of a new century and everything has changed, nothing remains the same. I had to sell father's estate, the house and gardens where I worked for so many years. Marie found a place for us to stay on the outskirts of town where I can see Monte Sainte Victoire in the distance. I have begun another painting of the familiar landscape that shows yellow orange rooftops flattened out against the dark green trees and a steel gray sky above the distant promontory. It is the same wonderful motif as before but my perception of the mountain is now entirely different. Nature itself has melted away, leaving only the colors and shapes to shimmer in the sunlight. To some it may seem chaotic but to me each object is connected to every other one.

In a world that trembles on the edge of disorder I still seek order and symmetry in my work. I still try to express the intensity of sensation that is unfolding before my eyes, although any improvement in my comprehension of nature is now accompanied by old age and a weakening of the body. Sometimes my mind can no longer distinguish between memory and fact, between reality and impression. It seems like only yesterday that I first met Hortense and brought her to the country house where Camille and I worked together. Pissarro is gone now. So is my old friend Emile. Everything passes with a terrifying rapidity.

Marie and I do not get along very well, but I am attempting to paint her portrait. She sits at an angle in front of a gold curtain, one hand resting on her knee and the other holding a thin yellow book. She appears to be sad, with a vacant stare and resigned look. Her dress is several shades of blue with a large bustle and flowered bonnet. I have decided to call it *Woman in Blue*. "When will you be finished?" she says, scowling. "There are other things I must attend to." Like father and Hortense, she is unable to concentrate on the moment or enjoy the simple pleasures of her surroundings. We have nothing in common and yet we must share the daily routine of our lives. Thank God Paul still comes here to help catalogue my work

I go every day to the river, to a place where the trees form a vault over the water. The light there is golden, the earth redolent of moisture and decay mingled with the smell of vegetation and newly mown fields nearby. I set up my easel and lay out my paints. Then I sit and stare at the tall arc of trees, their dark trunks clotted with lichen, the boughs of dappled leaves shining in the sunlight and bending toward the water below. The river itself is placid, reflecting the myriad shapes of trees and billowing clouds above. It is a familiar scene from my youth and my eyes are delighted by such glorious sensations. I could be happy just looking at these motifs forever without painting or changing my place, simply moving my head a little to the right or left. I still long to capture the elusive beauty of nature, to distill its essence for others to see. I allow the texture of the canvas to show through. Maurice Denis says it is a reminder that paintings are merely a flat surface covered with colors arranged in a certain way. Denis comes to see me regularly now, along with the others. It seems I have achieved some degree of recognition in my old age.

*

Paul has gone to live in Paris. It is just as well, since my health is failing and I had to hide my infirmities from him. My prickly skin is so sensitive that I can no longer bear for anyone to touch me. Father was like this just before his death. Once, when I grabbed his arm in anger, he cried out as if his flesh was on fire. Poor father, I can see him still, sitting alone in that stifling room. We are more alike than I ever would have thought. When I look in the mirror, each morning I see his sunken hollow cheeks and his wispy strands of hair. Marie says I have his disposition, having turned to religion as he did in old age. Perhaps it is the fear of what lies beyond or guilt over the sinful pleasures of my youth that make me feel this way, but I take no comfort in the stilted words of the local priest. Reason and morality are the enemy of art. The intense physical sensations of nature precede any attempt by science or religion to explain their meaning.

In morning, I stare at the white winter sky and look for some proof of God's existence but find none. I try again to see beyond the wall of nature, but instead I see only a blank canvas and feel compelled to fill it. For the sky, I create a patchwork of grays and whites and blues. Below that, a rocky landscape of browns and greens. Soon rocks fill the entire scene, like great slabs of cut stone. In front of them long diagonal trunks of pine trees in lavender and white and black. The painting is an opaque surface of shapes and colors and textures, not unlike nature itself. The white shows through in several places and that pleases me very much. Winter passes into spring, spring into summer, and still I have not completed the large painting of nude bathers. I am haunted by the vivid images of my youth which return now with astonishing clarity. I recall that sunny day on the riverbank with the country boys and their tales of naked girls. The canvas is almost finished, except for the figures. Will they be male or female this time?

I think of all the people I have painted over the years. Father and Hortense, Paul and Marie, the card players and the bathers. They are all mine now. I have captured them entirely in my mind and in my art. The painting has changed, the easel has moved, but the canvas remains the same. The only thing that matters is the inner life, what I feel inside and the reality that I perceive. For me, now, there is only the present and a vague sense of uneasiness. How distant everything seems and yet how close. The pain has returned again, the intense inner pain of being alone and of being a failure. I have always felt that way, but now more than ever. Only my work can distract me and help overcome the pain. Soon, perhaps, it will all be over.

Yesterday at the river a cold autumn rain began to fall. I felt the chill in my bones and was overcome by coughing and dizziness. Two workmen put me in a carriage and drove me home in the rain. When they lifted me I could smell the damp wool of their clothes and manure on their boots. They put me in a laundry cart and wheeled me into the house through the back door, past the pantry and into the front hall. Marie was furious at them for tracking mud on her carpet and continued to fuss while they carried me upstairs. She followed and told them to strip off my wet clothes before putting me into bed, where I lay coughing and shivering until she brought me hot tea.

When I drift off to sleep, the sight of the river is still fresh in my mind. I close my eyes and I am there again with the bathers, swinging out on the vine in a wide arc over the water, my companions staring up at my naked body in the sunlight. For just a second I am suspended high above the river of my youth. It is a moment of pure sweet ecstasy just before the release, when I plunge into the dark swirling water below.

Crap Shoot

The destination on the Number 8 streetcar said *Paradise*, but Sam Marinelli was going through hell. He missed his regular trolley and had to run several blocks to get the Number 8 instead. Paradise Avenue was a turnaround in West Baltimore but he was only going as far as downtown. Drenched with sweat, he stood in the aisle clinging to an overhead strap. The windows were open but no breeze entered the crowded streetcar as it crept along Pratt Street. When they came to a halt, the motorman clanged his bell loudly and Sam looked at the long line of cars ahead, their black roofs shimmering in the noonday sun. Today was a special day and he needed to get to work as soon as possible, so he decided to walk the last few blocks. He made his way to the front of the car and hopped down onto the street.

At the next corner he shaded his eyes against the dazzling

sunlight, trying to catch sight of his friend, Ted O'Neil, who directed traffic along the waterfront. Clouds of black smoke billowed from ships docked along Light Street but there was no sign of the stocky policeman. Sam took out a handkerchief to wipe the sweat from his forehead and neck. He should have brought a clean shirt for that night. If everything went as planned, he would propose to his sweetheart, Margaret, after his job tending bar at the Southern Hotel. Suddenly a large shadow fell across the street in front of him. He looked up to see a huge object looming above the Baltimore Trust Building. It was moving slowly but getting bigger as it crept over the skyscraper. He stared in disbelief as it completely blocked out the sun.

Two blocks away Ted O'Neil looked up and saw it, too, as all traffic came to a halt around him. Cars, trucks and streetcars stopped in their tracks while drivers gaped at the sight. Curious passengers emptied into the streets to see what was happening. People swarmed out of buildings to catch a glimpse of the strange airship hovering over the city. Few of them had bothered to read a small item in the morning paper about the German dirigible *Hindenburg* that was scheduled to land in New Jersey that afternoon. Even if they had, no one could have anticipated it would appear in the sky over Baltimore. When a thunder storm prevented it from landing as scheduled in New Jersey, the captain decided to head south and give his passengers a glimpse of the nation's capital. It flew over Atlantic City, the Eastern Shore of Maryland, and downtown Baltimore before reaching Washington, where it circled above the dome of the Capitol with the black and red swastika of the Nazi party emblazoned on its tail. The *Hindenburg* was the largest man-made object ever to fly. At more than 800 feet in length, it was only 78 feet shorter than the Titanic. When it flew from Germany to America the previous year in just sixty-two hours, newspapers praised the lighter-than-air ship and said that a new era of trans-Atlantic travel had begun.

"Did you see it?" Sam asked Ted O'Neil when the stocky policeman came into the hotel bar after work.

O'Neil removed his hat and mopped his brow. "Of course I saw it. How could you miss it?" He ordered a double shot of whiskey straight up. "It was up there for almost an hour," he said. "People left their cars to get a better view. Some were afraid it was going to drop a bomb. It took me an hour to get traffic back to normal thanks to those damned Nazis." He downed his drink in one gulp and asked for another.

When other regulars came into the bar, conversation turned to the upcoming presidential election. Franklin Roosevelt was running for a second term, and Baltimore always voted solidly Democratic. Roosevelt was a popular choice when he first ran in 1932, but now critics were accusing him of trying to spread socialism in America. The Knights of Columbus urged their members not to vote for Roosevelt, but Sam had decided to vote for FDR again. "He's a communist," Ted said when someone mentioned the president's name. "All his programs are steering us toward communism. As a Catholic, I can't in good conscience vote for him." He shook his head and downed his second drink.

"I admire the way he overcame polio," Sam said.

"Another reason not to vote for him. He doesn't have the stamina to run the government if we go to war with Germany."

Despite their differences, Sam liked the friendly cop whose father had come from Ireland and worked for the B&O Railroad. Ted had two sisters. The oldest girl was in the convent, but the other one was still at home. Her name was Margaret, and Ted had often hinted that she would be a good match for Sam. "She's a lovely Irish lass and I want you to meet her," he said before arranging their first date. Sam took Margaret to the premiere of "Gone with the Wind" at the Hippodrome Theater and they dated for almost a year before he decided to pop the question. Tonight was the big night, so he asked Ted to bring Margaret downtown to meet him after work.

Ted's eyes lit up. "What's the occasion?"

Sam winked at his friend. "We're going dancing in the rooftop ballroom."

The Rainbow Ballroom of the Southern Hotel was a large dimly lit room on the fifteenth floor with a stunning view of the city and harbor. As they rode up in the elevator, Sam admired Margaret's black sequin dress, her clear blue eyes, and the way she wore her auburn hair in a wave. "You look lovely tonight," he said and his heart leapt when she smiled at him. At the entrance to the ballroom he nodded to a waiter friend, who led them to a table by the windows. The band played several swing tunes before Sam asked Margaret to dance and held her close during a medley of Cole Porter songs. "What's your favorite?" he asked. "Mine is 'So in Love with You' from *Kiss Me Kate*."

"In the Still of the Night," she said softly. When the band played it, Sam looked into her eyes and sang along with the lyrics. *Do you love me, as I love you? Are you my life to be, my dream come true?* Then he kissed her on the cheek, inhaling the lilac perfume she often wore. At the end of the song he got down on one knee and proposed to her right there on the dance floor. Margaret blushed as band members and other couples applauded. Her eyes glistened in the soft light, but she said nothing.

Confused and disappointed, Sam led her back to the table. Ted had warned him she was a strong-willed woman, but that was one of the things he liked about her. He thought back over their previous dates, wondering if he had been too forward or stepped out of line. Once, lying on the grass beneath the stars in Druid Hill Park, they had kissed long and ardently, leaving them both flushed and breathless. But he had never done it again, content to wait until their wedding night to pursue his passion. Now they sat in silence while he waited for her to say something. Finally, Margaret looked at him and said, "Sam, you are the dearest, kindest man I've ever met. Of course I'll marry you."

Sam smiled and took her hand. He had never felt so happy. Gazing out the window at the lights below, he thought about the giant airship that had flown over the city that day. It must be amazing to fly in something that soars so high above the earth, something lighter than air. That's how he felt now with Margaret, lighter than air.

They were married the following spring, not long after the *Hindenburg* crashed and burned. Ted O'Neil said the disaster was an omen of terrible things to come, and he was right. By 1940, the year of the first peacetime draft, Sam and Margaret were the proud parents of a two year old girl named Marie and there were plenty of other young men to serve their country. But in the days and weeks following the Japanese attack on Pearl Harbor, millions of men enlisted or were drafted, including Sam and his friend Lucky.

Lucky's real name was Luciano Ibolito, but everyone called him Lucky because he was good at shooting craps. On New

Year's Eve, after passing their Army physical at Fort Holabird, Sam and Lucky were shooting craps in the back room of a dry cleaning shop in Little Italy. "Come on seven," Lucky said, breathing heavily on the dice. He had been winning more than the others, as usual, but this time he rolled a three and lost. "Let's go, Sammy," he said. "It's time for lunch and I'm buying." The other players howled in protest but Lucky ignored them.

He and Sam walked down Exeter Street to their favorite pizza parlor. "I really like this place," Lucky said after they had ordered. "Maybe I'll win it in a craps game someday."

"I want to buy a pair of dice before we leave for boot camp," Sam said. "And I'd like you to help me pick them out."

Lucky smiled. "I know this pawn shop over on Eastern Avenue that's got a good selection."

At his friend's urging, Sam bought a pair of pure white ivories. He paid more than he intended but they came in a little brown pouch with a drawstring. It would be the only pair of dice he ever owned. As they came out of the pawn shop Lucky pointed to the Navy recruiting office across the street. "I just got an idea," he said. "Life is a crap shoot, so why not take our best shot?" Sam followed him and they enlisted in the United States Navy just two days before their Army draft notices came in the mail.

After six grueling weeks of basic training in Norfolk, Sam was assigned to a ship bound for the South Pacific while Lucky was sent to the North Atlantic. When they said goodbye at Camden Station, each carried his own pair of dice. Sam boarded a train bound for Chicago while Lucky left on another train for Philadelphia. Thousands of old passenger cars had been painted olive green and put back into service as troop carriers. Despite the bitter cold, the inside of the steel coach was hot and smelly. On the long ride to Chicago, Sam slept on a wool seat that reeked of sweat and relieved himself in a tiny lavatory where the toilet emptied onto the tracks below. In Chicago, he boarded a second train for the rest of the trip to San Diego. This one was even worse than the first, the steel car so hot and the roaches so thick that he could hardly sleep. As they crossed the Great Salt Lake, his seat mate caught one, pulled out his pen knife, and sliced it in half. "Look at this son of a bitch," he said, laughing. "The insides are all white." Sam turned away and looked out the window at the brilliant white salt flats that stretched endlessly toward the horizon. He didn't believe in cruelty, even to the lowest form of life, and wondered how he would survive the war if he had to see a single human death.

In San Diego he reported for duty on an LST landing craft, a long narrow ship that transported Marines and equipment to the beachheads during an invasion. Lying in his cramped bunk on the first night at sea, he stared at the bulkhead pockmarked with rivets and recalled the newsreels of ships burned or sunk at Pearl Harbor. For the first time since enlisting he was afraid. Before falling asleep he rubbed the little pouch of dice for good luck and thought of the lighter-than-air feeling on the night he proposed to Margaret. He slept fitfully that night, his dreams mingled with the throbbing of the engines.

In the morning he awoke with a headache and his stomach churned as the LST lurched between heavy swells. Later that day, while swabbing the deck in the hot afternoon sun, he felt sick to his stomach. An officer noticed and pointed to the stern, where Sam hung his head over the railing with several others and heaved up his lunch. Then he went below to help prepare the evening meal.

As a Ship's Cook Third Class, Sam spent endless hours each day stirring fifty gallon containers of soup, boiling potatoes by the hundreds, and shoveling flour into a giant mixer to make dough. When they reached their first destination in the South Pacific, the nearest battleship in the convoy was a thousand yards away but from the galley below he could hear the 16mm guns open fire. After they fell silent he heard the call to general quarters and reported to his battle station on deck. Whistles sounded, an officer barked orders, and the Marines prepared to go ashore. It was the same everywhere they landed: the terrible pounding of big guns from the battleships followed by the frightened look on the faces of men preparing to go ashore.

Sam spent his days serving troops in the tight spaces of the galley and sharing cigarettes or stories of home with them on the heaving deck of the ship. Then, as he watched them leave, he wondered who would die and who would survive. During his twenty-two months in the South Pacific, he never saw an enemy soldier first hand, never stared death in the face, and never had to kill another human being, but he saw the carnage left behind by those who did. Once, in the early light of dawn, he caught a glimpse of what looked like driftwood or dried seaweed on the beach. Then the morning haze lifted like a curtain and he saw clearly that the dark clumps scattered in the sand were the bodies of dead Marines. Often in his sleep he heard their agonized screams or saw their lifeless eyes staring at the sky. And he prayed for them every night. *Sweet Jesus, have mercy on their souls.*

Sam was lucky. After two years at sea, he was reassigned to the naval base in Norfolk to help train new recruits. From there he was able to visit Margaret and their four year old daughter in Baltimore. When they slept together again for the first time, he told her about his nightmares and the images of death burned into his mind. She held him close and he felt comfort in her warm embrace. They made ardent love and she conceived a second child, Frankie, who was born the following summer. Unlike Sam, Lucky was badly injured when his ship was hit by enemy aircraft in the North Sea. He was sent home with a shattered leg that was replaced by a steel one at the Veterans' Hospital and he walked with a serious limp for the rest of his life. After the war Sam often invited Lucky to dinner at their house. He entertained the kids by poking a hat pin into his fake leg while they stared at him with wide-eyed amazement. To them it looked like magic or else a miracle. Despite his handicap Lucky became a familiar sight on the streets of downtown Baltimore as an organ grinder with a trained monkey that danced at his feet and collected coins tossed on the sidewalk by passing shoppers.

As fate would have it, Sam was home on leave the day Japan surrendered. He and Margaret took their family to St. Leo's in Little Italy to say a prayer of thanks. They carried Frankie inside with them but Marie was afraid of the dark interior so they left her on the front steps with a neighbor. As they knelt in a pew near the entrance, Sam looked up at the stained glass windows that depicted scenes from the life of Christ. One showed the crucifixion with Roman soldiers rolling dice to determine who would get the robe worn by Jesus. The dice puzzled Sam because there were three, not the two used in most games of chance that he knew. He recalled what Lucky said the day they enlisted and realized that it was true. *Life is a crap shoot.* He could have been killed in the war like so many others or come back with a shattered leg like his friend. Sam had clung to his faith during those terrible days in the South Pacific and he still believed in heaven, but after what he had seen in the war it seemed to him that people suffered enough here on earth without being punished again in the next life.

His thoughts were interrupted by the sound of Marie screaming. He rushed outside to see her pointing up at a Navy airship nosing its way over the steeple. Sam smiled and took her in his arms. "Don't be afraid," said. "It's only a blimp."

That evening, thirty miles to the south, Harry Truman walked to the White House gates with his wife and waived at the crowds in Lafayette Park. When he announced a week earlier that the first atomic bomb had been dropped on Hiroshima, Truman called it a military target. But the country soon learned that eighty thousand civilians had been killed there, most of them incinerated in a single flash of nuclear death. In Baltimore that night there was music and celebration. People gathered in the streets of Little Italy to hug one another, pop champagne bottles, and dance in the streets. Sam and Margaret watched as a man with a trumpet climbed onto the roof of a car and played "Auld Lang Syne." The sweet sadness of the melody played on a solitary trumpet reminded him of his buddies lost at sea or gunned down on the beaches. When the song ended, many in the crowd were moved to tears, including Sam. Later, as he walked home with his arm around Margaret, he sensed that their life had changed somehow, that this was the end of one thing and the beginning of something else. He remembered how Lucky often said that life is a crap shoot and wondered what the future would bring.

Hole in the Ground

A One-Act Play

TIME: The recent past

SETTING: A country cemetery

CHARACTERS: Norm: early-sixties, tall and thin, very talkative

Bert: mid-fifties, short and stocky, a bit slow

Lil: Norm's wife, in her late-fifties

SCENE 1

The lights come up on Norm and Bert sitting on a mound
of dirt, eating their lunch. Their picks and shovels lie on the
ground nearby.

NORM: You been fishin' lately, Bert?

BERT: Nope.

NORM: *He munches on a sandwich.* Lots of worms in that last hole. We should've saved 'em for bait. *Pause.* Everything alright at home?

BERT: Yup.

NORM: Lil and I went to a movie last night. Some stupid-ass film about people comin' back from the dead. Lil liked it but I didn't. Seems like everything these days is about ghosts or vampires. *Pause.* Heard an interview on the radio with this guy. Some kind of writer. Said he was writin' three plays about death. A *tril-o-gy*, he called it. The first one was about dyin', what happens when the body has an illness with no chance of recovery. The second one was about how the body gets embalmed before a funeral. How they suck out the organs before pumpin' in the fluid. Sounded really disgusting. But here's the weird part. He said he was savin' the third one till he finds out what happens after death. *Pause.* Now I ask you, Bert, how could he do that? He'd be dead, for Chris' sake.

BERT: *Puzzled.* Yup.

NORM: *He finishes the sandwich.* Watched this TV show the other night, one of those *doc-u-men-tary* things. Learned a new word: *in-hu-ma-tion.* It means buryin' the dead like we do instead of disposin' of the body some other way, like cree-mation. *Pause.* Did you know there are some places where people used to bury the dead under their livin' room floor or else eat the bodies of their ancestors? Sounds awful, don't it? Inhuman almost. *He pauses with a puzzled look on his face.* Anyhow, they showed a cemetery in Paris where they had to dig up the dead from long ago because the bodies had decayed and the churchyard was sinkin' into the ground so stench from the bodies filled the whole neighborhood. What did they expect to happen, for Chris' sake? This was before they started puttin' people into metal boxes and concrete vaults like they do now to stop the body from decomposing. *Pause.* I never thought about it before, but that's the natural order of things, ain't it? The way it's been for thousands of years. Flesh feedin' the worms. Bones fertilizin' the earth. *Pause.* I remember readin' history books back in school about kings and queens, armies and generals, and how the common people always suffered the most. If you ask me, there's no such thing as history. Just corpses rottin' away in the earth, like ruins from the past. That's the way things are supposed to be. When you're gone you're gone. It's that simple. Dead is dead. *Pause.* That's what I told Lil when we talked about who would die first. You'll survive, I said. Life goes on 'cause it's all we have. *Pause.* You know I'm not a religious man, Bert. Never have been, so that's what I believe.

BERT: Yup.

NORM: Watched this other *doc-u-men-tary* that made no sense at all. About somethin' called a black hole up in space, if you can imagine that. And it sucks everything into it.

BERTZ: *Puzzled.* Where's it go?

NORM: That's the thing. Nobody knows for sure, but they say it could suck in the whole solar system. Can you imagine that? The whole solar system goin' into this immense black hole that nobody can see because it's invisible?

BERT: I don't understand. What's their point in sayin' somethin' like that?

NORM: *He glances at Bert.* Careful, Bert. That was two sentences you just strung together. Don't want to tax yourself too much. *Pause.* What's the point? Well, the point is, do they really expect us to believe crap like that? I mean, don't we have enough to worry about already? Getting' up every day, trudgin' off to work. Breakin' our backs, barely earnin' enough to feed our face, goin' home to the wife at night, eatin' our daily bread, then sittin' down to hear some pointy-head scientist say we're all goin' to be sucked into a giant hole in space that nobody can even see? *He gestures toward the empty grave behind them.* That's where we're all goin' to end up. A hole in the ground.

BERT: *He nods.* Yup.

NORM: *He closes his lunch box.* You know, some people think that because we dig graves all day, we must talk a lot about death. We do sometimes, I guess, but not all the time.

BERT: Nope.

NORM: Look here, Bert. Time for me to wring out the hose, if you get my drift. I'm goin' over there behind that big oak tree, if you care to join me.

BERT: No, thanks.

NORM: I won't be long. *He exits off right.*
Bert watches Norm leave. Then he grins and goes around behind the mound. After a minute, a skull rises slowly above the mound. Laughter is heard as Bert manipulates the skull on a pole so that it turns from side to side and looks around . The skull disappears quickly just before Norm returns. Norm sits on the mound, looks around for Bert, and shakes his head. When the skull rises again and looks at him, Norm speaks without glancing at it.

NORM: Bert, what the hell are you doin'?

BERT: *Laughing.* Just havin' a bit of fun.

NORM: What if someone comes along? Like a little kid or some old lady? You'd scare the crap out of 'em. You've had your fun, so come on back here and finish your lunch.
The skull disappears and Bert comes back. He sits on the mound and eats an apple. There is a moment of silence before Norm speaks again.

NORM: That skull once had a tongue in it and could sing.

BERT: What?

NORM: I said that skull once had a tongue in it and could sing.

BERT: *Puzzled.* What did it sing?

NORM: Whatever it wanted to when it was young and happy. But when it got older, probably somethin' sad. *Pause.* How's the arthritis, Bert? Mine's killin' me and all this diggin' only makes it worse. Maybe someday they'll get us one of those machines, the kind that digs trenches. *Pause.* But then they'd have to teach us how to use it, wouldn't they? And that could be a problem. I mean, what if we made a mistake with the gears and the machine hit one of us in the head or ran over us? *He shrugs.* Guess I'm just a pick and shovel man myself. How 'bout you?

BERT: *He nods.* Yup.

Bert gets up suddenly, his face contorted in pain. He grabs his stomach and looks at Norm.

NORM: What's wrong, Bert? Bowel problems again?

BERT: *He nods his head vigorously.* Yup.

NORM: It's a long walk back to the john. Think you can make it?

BERT: *He shakes his head with a look of panic.* Nope.

NORM: Jesus, if you're that desperate go and use the grave we just dug. *He gestures behind the mound.* It's just a hole in the ground. *Bert nods and disappears behind the mound.*

NORM: *Shouting.* Just be sure to cover it up with a shovel full of dirt. *He laughs.* Wouldn't want to spoil someone's funeral, would we?

Norm whistles to himself until Bert returns.

NORM: Never had that happen before, did we?

BERT: Nope.

NORM: You're such a talker, Bert. A real *con-ver-sa-tion-ist.*

BERT: *He shrugs.* I try.

NORM: That's what I told Lil the other night. Old Bert's always talkin' his head off. There's not a moment's peace for me, even among the dead. *Pause.* I don't know why, but I been thinkin' a lot about the hereafter lately and what people think it's like. Some folks say you just go on rememberin' what you did here on earth. *Pause.* Been thinkin' a lot about Lil, too, wonderin' what she'll do after I'm gone.

BERT: You sick, Norm?

NORM: No. Just gettin' old I guess. *Pause.* Think I'll take Lil out for dinner this weekend.

BERT: *Puzzled.* Why?

NORM: Just to show her I care, that's all. *He looks around.* Well, time to move on. Find out where the next hole's supposed to be and start diggin'. *He gets up and rubs his back.* Jesus, my back's killin' me.

 They gather up their tools and leave. The lights dim briefly to indicate a passage of time.

SCENE 2

 The lights get brighter as Lil enters carrying a small wooden box. She looks around, sees the mound of dirt, and glances behind it at the empty grave. Then she comes back to face the audience.

LIL: Well, Norm, I brung the ashes. *Pause.* The man at the funeral home said they're called *cree-mains*. I think that's a funny word, one you'd probably laugh at. When you first mentioned it, I didn't understand why you wanted it this way. But once you explained it to me, it made sense. No embalmment, no viewing of your body, no rotting away inside a metal box. Good thing I'm not religious, though, or I'd be worried about what some folks call the resurrection of the body. *Pause.* I guess dead's just dead, like you always said.

It was really sweet of you to take me out to dinner the other night. Who would've guessed you'd choke to death on a fish bone. It all happened so fast. The waiter did his best to save you and the owner felt really bad about it afterwards. *Pause.* Everyone at the service was so nice, especially your friend Bert. You were right, though. He's a man of few words. When the service was over I told him what you died from and he started laughing. He laughed himself silly all the way out the door.

I hope you feel comfortable here where you spent so many days working. Remember how I used to ask what it was like to work among all these gravestones? You laughed and said it was just a job. But sometimes in your sleep you'd say the strangest things, like you was talking to the dead, asking them what it was like. *She wipes away a tear and looks around.* Now that I'm here, though, I'm not sure where to put the ashes. You said to scatter them around, but I don't like that 'cause the wind might carry them away. *She walks to the edge of the mound and looks at the empty grave.* Maybe in that hole back there, even though it belongs to someone else. *She looks around again and sees the oak tree off right.* Or I could dig a hole under that big oak tree. *She smiles.* And I could carve our initials in the tree, just like I did when we were young. You remember, don't you Norm? A heart with our initials and the word *Forever.* It seems like only yesterday even though it was a long time ago. *Pause.* But I don't have a knife with me and some dog might come along and piss on you under the tree. So I guess it has to be the empty grave after all.

She goes behind the mound and pours the contents of the box into the grave. Then she comes back and faces the audience again.

LIL: That hole smells real nasty, Norm. *She sighs.* I don't know

how you did it, comin' out here day after day for so long. *She shudders.* Cemeteries are such creepy places. I never told you that, but I hate them. *Pause.* There's a hole inside of me, Norm, and I don't know how I'll ever fill it. It's even bigger than the hole I poured your ashes in. *She sighs.* I guess I'll get used to it somehow. I remember what you said to me once. *You'll survive. Life goes on because it's all we got. She smiles.* It's funny not hearin' you say anything back to me, though. You always had somethin' to say about everything. I guess I'll get used to that, too. *Pause.* I can't think of nothin' else to say, except I love you. But you know that, don't you? I hope you know 'cause I sure as hell won't be comin' back here again. *She looks at the empty box.* I bet you knew that all along, didn't you? This was just your way of makin' sure I'd let go once and for all. *She glances back toward the grave.* Well, there you are, Norm. *Pause.* Goodbye, love.
She turns and walks off slowly. When the stage is empty, the lights fade to black.

How the Dead Are Buried

In the summer following their freshman year of high school, Tommy and Iggy were lying out at the Patterson Park pool on their stomachs to hide the boners they got from watching the girls go by. Tommy closed his eyes and felt the hot sun beating down on his back. He listened to the shouts of children splashing in the water until he heard a funny noise and opened his eyes. Iggy was making armpit farts at a thin blond girl with circles under her eyes. She stopped to stare at him, wide eyed, then gave him the finger and moved on.

"Who was that?" Tommy asked.

"Rose Gorelski, known as Rosie the Rosebud. She's easy, if you know what I mean."

Tommy nodded, pretending to know what his friend was talking about. He hated it when Iggy had to explain things like that to him and wondered where he learned about them.

Rosie Gorelski walked by again after Iggy went to the snack bar. Tommy couldn't help staring at her bleached blond hair and brightly painted red toenails. She turned and glared at him. "What are you looking at, you little dick?"

Tommy was mortified and looked away until she left. Then he saw Barbara Orlinsky coming out of the bath house in her bikini. He shut his eyes, pretending to be asleep, until she got closer. Then he opened one eye and saw a mole on the inside of her thigh. As she passed closer, he opened both eyes and watched her hips swaying rhythmically above the narrow crotch of her pink bikini. The hot sun burned right through his body to the boner throbbing beneath him. Suddenly, unable to control what was happening, he shot his wad right there at the pool. "Oh, shit," he moaned out loud and buried his head in the towel.

"What's wrong?" Iggy asked when he came back.

Without raising his head Tommy said, "I lost it, Igg. I got a boner watching Barbara Orlinsky go by and shot my wad. What am I gonna do?"

Iggy looked at him. "Don't move. Whatever you do, don't move. Just lie there until I get back." Then he ran to the other side of the pool.

Tommy watched Iggy disappear into the bath house. He was so embarrassed that he couldn't think straight, but he did what his friend said because he didn't dare to move. When he heard bare feet slapping the wet concrete, he looked up to see Iggy standing over him with a bucket full of water. Instinctively, he rolled over to avoid being doused. As he did, Iggy dumped the cold water onto his crotch. Tommy howled. His trunks were soaking wet, but his problem was solved.

They had grown up together in East Baltimore, riding

their bikes down to the waterfront in Canton and along Boston Street to Fells Point. They played basketball at the Rec Center and baseball in Patterson Park. In the eighth grade Tommy was an altar boy at Saint Elizabeth's while Iggy sang in the church choir. To everyone's surprise, Iggy sang with a clear soprano voice that sounded like an angel. Old ladies cried and young girls swooned when he opened his mouth to sing. They forgot his foul language, his snickering laugh, and his crooked teeth. The choir director always picked him to sing the *Ave Maria* at funerals and the *Panis Angelicus* at First Holy Communion. But the boys teased Iggy about it, saying, "You better watch out. One day your voice will change and they'll cut off your balls just to keep you in the choir."

Iggy's father was an undertaker, and the Zeiler family lived on the second floor of a corner row house above the funeral home. The neighbors said that Mr. Zeiler embalmed corpses down in the basement and Tommy once asked Iggy if he had ever watched his father work. "Oh, yeah," he said. "My dad's stuck his hands into all kinds of things." Then, with a loud staccato laugh, he added, "Don't ever go rummaging around in our garbage cans."

Iggy often got into fights with the other guys who ragged him about his father's business. Eddie Rybcynski liked to tease him by asking, "Hey Iggy, your old man ever do it with a corpse?" One day Frank Lancelotta said, "What's that stink coming from your chimney? Did your old man cremate some-one last night?"

Iggy yelled back at him. "It's no worse than the smell from your sister's snatch." Then he went after Chuck with fists fly-ing until they both ended up on the ground with bloody noses.

Later that summer, on a sweltering July afternoon, Tommy

celebrated his sixteenth birthday with Iggy in the alley behind the funeral parlor. They sat on the warm concrete with their backs against a chain link fence and drank a six-pack from Mr. Zeiler's walk-in refrigerator down in the basement. Tommy was afraid to ask what else was stored there. After his second beer, he confessed to Iggy that he had a crush on Barbara Orlinsky.

"No shit." Iggy rolled his eyes and took a swig of beer.

Tommy looked at the sealed trash cans in the Zeiler's back yard. "Does your old man really embalm corpses?"

Iggy nodded. "When I saw him do it the first time, I ran into the john and puked. But by the time we were in eighth grade I was helping out."

Tommy had suspected as much but was still surprised. "What do you do?"

"Simple stuff, like stripping the body and moving the stretcher into place. Then I hand him the tools when he's ready to start. I could probably do it by myself now, except that would be illegal." He glanced at Tommy. "Sure you want to hear this, sport?"

"Yup."

"First thing we do is slide the naked corpse from the stretcher onto a stainless steel table."

Tommy stared at him. "The first time you did it, was it a man or a woman?"

Iggy blinked. "The first time was a woman."

"So you got to see her naked body?"

"She was dead, for Chris' sake. It ain't the same as what you see in *Playboy*. Besides, they're mostly old and shriveled up. Especially when we're done with them." Iggy let out his loud staccato laugh.

Tommy took another swig of beer. "What next?" He was dying to know but afraid to hear the gory details.

"We drain all the blood out from an artery at the same time we inject chemicals into another artery." Iggy took a swig of beer. "Sometimes I have to hold an arm or a leg down so the blood drains out properly while my old man does the injection." He looked at Tommy. "You all right, sport?"

"Yeah, I'm okay. Then what?"

"Then we do the cavity. That's the fun part. My old man cuts a hole in the stomach and inserts this long metal tube with a suction hose attached to it. That sucks out all the gas and fluids and stuff from the organs so we can pump the chemicals in."

Tommy was starting to feel queasy. "What do you do with all the stuff that comes out?"

"If it's liquid, it goes down the drain into the sewer. If it's solid, it goes into a special tank that gets emptied once a month." He paused. "You ready for the last part?"

Tommy finished his beer. Everything was starting to look green. "Sure, why not?"

"My old man sews up the holes he made in the body while I massage the face and hands with a special cream to make them soft. Then he puts cotton in the nose and mouth and eyelids. Sometimes up the ass and in the vagina, too. For some really bad cases, he has to stuff cotton down the throat and then wire the mouth shut."

Tommy eyes grew wide and his stomach was churning. "Does the body, like, move at all while you're doing this?"

"Nah. The rigor mortis has set in by then and they're usually stiff as a board." He paused. "Sometimes, if they had arthritis really bad, my old man has to cut through a muscle or tendon so the hands and arms look natural in the casket."

Memories of his grandmother's viewing ran through Tommy's head. He had been afraid to look at her face, so he stared at the white satin lining inside the coffin and then at the gnarled fingers with a rosary wrapped around them.

"The last thing we do is put the clothes on and apply make-up. That's my favorite part. It's what my old man let me do first and it's really cool, except when you have to glue the fingers together. Everything has to look perfect, you know, like the person is just sleeping and not really dead. Like they're still alive in the same room with you."

Tommy was feeling woozy. He wanted to ask something else but had trouble remembering what. "How do you…?"

Iggy smiled, as if he knew what Tommy was thinking. "I pretend they're mummies, that's all. Just friggin' mummies. That's how I get through it."

"Thanks, Igg'. I really 'ppreciate your tellin' me this."

But Iggy wasn't finished. "My old man explained to me once how embalming started with the Egyptians. Before they could be mummified all the internal organs had to be removed, just like we do. Except for one big difference." He glanced at Tommy. "You okay, sport? You gonna pass out on me?"

Bleary eyed, Tommy shook his head and waited for Iggy to continue.

"The Egyptians also removed the dead person's brain. Know how they did that?"

Tommy didn't answer. His head was spinning and he suddenly felt faint.

"They pulled it out with a long hook through the nose."

Tommy heard his friend's loud staccato laugh as the chain link fence pressed sharply into his back. He struggled to stay upright, to keep from getting sick, but his mouth filled up with bile and he puked down the front of his shirt. Then he keeled over into Iggy's lap.

Two weeks later they were walking behind a short blond girl in flip flops on their way to Matthew's Pizza parlor. Tommy stared at her tan legs and the back of her tight denim skirt moving rhythmically as she walked. *Flip flop. Flip flop.* Then he imagined what the golden palace between her thighs looked like and felt himself getting hard. *Flip flop. Flip flop.*

Iggy looked at him and smiled. "You got a boner yet, sport? You gonna cream in your jeans?"

"Shut up, Iggy." Ever since he claimed to have gone all the way with a girl, Iggy annoyed Tommy with his constant teasing about sex.

"Are you still hung up on Barbara Orlinsky?"

Tommy winced. Sometimes Iggy could see right into his soul. He still dreamt about touching Barbara's breasts, but the most he ever managed to do was kiss her with his tongue. Once, at a party.

"You need to stop jerking off so much and get laid, pal. Want me to fix you up with someone?"

"You're sick, Iggy. Did I ever tell you that? All you think about is sex and corpses."

Iggy smirked. "What else is there?

Tommy stopped dead in his tracks, startled by what his friend said and by the thought of what he might have done. Iggy kept on walking but at the corner he glanced back and yelled, "Come on, asshole." Then he cocked his head and held his middle finger in the air. Tommy turned around and headed home.

They both went to Calvert Hall, a private Catholic high

school, but in the fall of their sophomore year Iggy flunked out. Poor at math and science, he had been in danger of flunking ever since they started. After Iggy transferred to public high school they slowly drifted apart. Tommy graduated with a scholarship to a college in Philadelphia while Iggy enlisted and went to Fort Bragg, North Carolina, for basic training.

Tommy finally got laid during his freshman year of college. He started dating a girl named Rose who invited him to drink beer with her friends one night in the woods behind campus. Tommy was still shy but he was delighted when Rose took the initiative. The next morning he remembered the girl called Rosey in Patterson Park and wondered what Iggy would say if he knew that Tommy finally had sex with a girl by the same name. They had lost touch with each other, but he heard that Iggy was part of Operation Desert Shield in Kuwait.

Tommy's mother called him one night before Christmas break with the news about Iggy's death. "I'm sorry you missed the funeral," she said. "But I just read about it in the church bulletin."

Tommy was so shaken that all he could do was mumble into the phone. "I wonder who embalmed him." There was a brief silence on the other end before his mother answered.

"I think they're sent home in a sealed coffin already embalmed."

Tommy was relieved despite the numbing sadness he felt. There was a time when he thought he and Iggy would be friends forever.

That night, after drowning his grief with Rose and her friends, he walked back to the dorm alone. In the darkness he heard a loud staccato laugh and whirled around but no one was there. Gazing up at the black sky filled with stars, he imagined

Iggy's flag draped casket at his family's funeral parlor, heard his angelic voice singing *Ave Maria* at the Requiem Mass, and recalled the last words uttered by the priest at the cemetery. *Ashes to ashes, dust to dust.* His heart surged and he suppressed a sob. Then, shrugging off the cold and tears, he turned back toward the dorm. He wished he had kept in touch. He wished that Iggy had never enlisted. Most of all he wished his friend had been cremated. Iggy would have liked it that way.

Pittsburgh Madonna

Andy Warhol was surprised when the nurses in the emergency room treated him like everyone else until he realized that no one recognized him because he was paler than usual and had lost so much weight. Or because he wasn't wearing his usual wig. When he left the apartment that morning, he was in such pain that he just grabbed a hat to cover his head.

At the hospital he told the doctors about the pain in his stomach. He told them about his eating habits and his last meal in the restaurant. Then he submitted his body to their probes and tests and sat alone in the curtained-off area to wait for the results. He heard the low moaning sound of someone else in pain and thought about the time, almost twenty years ago, when he was shot. A bullet had pierced his lung, esophagus, gall bladder, liver, and spleen. He still remembered the awful ride in the ambulance, the confusion in the emergency room, and his body being hooked up to machines. His chest and stomach were still a patchwork of scars and he hadn't been back to a hospital since. Not until today. He told himself that it wasn't as bad this time, but then the doctors returned to say that minor surgery was needed. They said it was a simple procedure and the only way to make the pain go away. But he was still afraid.

Later, beneath a white grid of fluorescent lights, Andy stared helplessly at the ceiling from a gurney as a sea of electric blue and hospital green swirled around him. He was wheeled into the operating room and a circular shape appeared above him, a pink face with an oval of blue over the mouth and nose. The anesthetist explained what she was going to do and then said, "Start counting backwards from one hundred, please." He stared at the upside down face when she said this and wondered if she recognized him. By now most of the staff had figured out who he was.

"How far should I count?" he asked.

"Most people only get to ninety," she said without looking at him. "Please start now." Her tone reminded him of the collagen girl who administered his monthly scalp treatments.

Andy knew what would happen when he lost consciousness. He knew where the images and memories would take him. He thought about how often he had taken that trip in his head only to emerge from the dark tunnel of gloom into the white daylight of conscious memory. Reluctantly he started counting.

"One hundred. Ninety-nine. Ninety-eight." Numbing darkness began to close in. He wanted to resist, to protest, but he couldn't. He opened his mouth to speak.

"Not quite right," he managed to say. "Too much contrast.

Re-shoot the negative." He was at the Factory, overseeing work on one of his favorite subjects but trying not to show any emotion in his voice. When his assistants were ready he had them pull the silk-screen again. This time the results were better, but still too dark. The next print was almost perfect, and the one after that was exactly what he wanted. As he watched, a life-size image of Elvis slowly emerged. He wore a holster and had a six-shooter in his right hand. The image was silver and black and somewhat faded, but otherwise it looked just like an old movie still. "We'll use that one," he said, "and then do one more exactly like it. Only one. No more." He called it *Single Elvis*, and saved the second print for his private collection. He would decide later what to do with it.

Andy's head was full of such images. They came from everywhere: things he remembered, things he clipped out of newspapers, things he photographed, even things people sent to him in the mail. Sometimes he sorted them out in his mind. Sometimes he drew them on paper until he got them right. "Save everything," Picasso's daughter once told him. "Then sell everything." He agreed completely, but he had to be careful. He didn't want anyone to know how much he was really worth, especially the IRS.

"Ninety-five, ninety-four, ninety-three" he heard his voice saying. He was on the train from New York to Pittsburgh. He could have gone by private limousine, but he liked trains. It was a ride backwards in time. They passed factories and steel mills along the way. He saw mechanics and workmen beside the tracks. He realized that he no longer worked with his hands. Instead he made money with his mind, with his imagination, with how he was able to manipulate images and colors. Critics said his work was the greatest breakthrough in art since the urinals of Marcel Duchamp. He felt smug about this. He felt superior. But he also felt things he didn't want to feel. He was frustrated by the vicious cycle of his life: he had achieved everything and yet he felt that he had nothing. He wanted to distance himself not only from the images of his childhood that he saw from the train but from the success of the present.

He sat very still for a long time and let the images stream past the window. Gradually he became conscious not of the objects passing by outside but only of the sense of movement they created, of the sunlight flickering on his lap. Then he felt calm again. His earliest childhood memory was of sitting on the floor with his mother in a patch of flickering sunlight. He felt ready to face his mother. She loved Elvis and he had brought a photo of Elvis with him.

Before senility set in, his mother had once told him exactly how she wanted the details of her funeral arranged. She wanted two days for viewing the body at the neighborhood funeral parlor with a guest book for all to sign. She wanted her rose petal rosary from the Vatican wrapped around her fingers in the coffin, and the *Ave Maria* to be sung when the pallbearers brought the body into church. She wanted everyone to be invited back to her sister's house for a meal after the burial. She was even specific about the food to be served: pierogi and kielbasa, bigos and cabbage. There was always the sweet, pungent smell of cooked cabbage in their house.

He was in a cab on his way to the funeral home. He passed through their old neighborhood. He saw the candy store where his mother used to take him for a Saturday morning treat and the elementary school where the halls always smelled of bubble gum. He passed the barbershop on the corner, its windows now shuttered with chain link and its rust colored bricks spray-painted with graffiti. Everything seemed faded and flat now, not at all like he had remembered it.

At the funeral parlor he moved past a cluster of mourners at the entrance and slowly made his way to the casket at the front of the room. His brothers were there but they pretended not to see him. When he saw what was left of his mother, he looked away from the sunken eyes, the pallid skin, and her gnarled fingers clasping the rosary. He stared instead at her flowery green dress and thought of the nickname she had once given him: A&W. Her favorite photograph of him as a child was of his first attempt to drink A&W root beer through a straw. She said his face was so full of happiness that he looked like an angel. He loved the soda and she loved the nickname.

For just a moment his eyes filled up and he was unable to breathe. He waited for the sob to subside and then looked around to discover that his brothers had seen to everything. Racks of flowers were neatly arranged behind the coffin and a podium stood at the back of the room with the guest book on it. There was even a little stack of holy cards on the kneeler next to the coffin. He took one of the cards and looked at it. On the front was his mother's name, the date of her death, and a prayer to the Virgin Mary. On the other side was a Byzantine image of the Madonna and Child that he recognized from the religious books his mother used to read to him as a child. There was something beautiful, serene and otherworldly about the figure of Mary, with her long thin fingers and large sympathetic eyes. Very carefully, Andy put the card in his wallet. He stood to one side of the coffin in his black suit, dark shades, and silver wig. He folded his hands and waited.

Eventually, people he hadn't seen in years came up to him, and said they were sorry about his mother. Some of them asked him what it was like to live in New York. No one in the family spoke to him. His brothers were more than content to leave him alone with his thoughts, which were mostly about how he could sneak the picture of Elvis into the coffin before it was closed.

During the funeral mass the church was filled with the smell of flowers and burning incense, reminding him of their Sunday afternoons together. They would walk home through the park after church and she would cook his favorite meal of cabbage with caraway seeds and onions. He sat stiffly staring at the closed coffin until the *Ave Maria* was sung, then he took out the holy card and stared at it. The colors were rich and shimmering, the folds of Mary's deep red dress surrounded by rays of gold that looked like sunbursts. The Christ child on her knee was clothed in royal blue, his right hand raised in benediction. Behind them was a procession of saints and above them angels hovered with layered wings of multicolored feathers.

At the cemetery the family waited on a bright green carpet for the others to crowd around the gravesite. Andy stared at the faded sky while the priest intoned the final prayers. Afterward they all rode in silence to his brother's house. While his sister-in-law was putting out the food, her kids started laughing at his wig. At first he pretended not to notice, then he took off his dark glasses and stared at them until they left. When his brother came into the dining room, Andy went over to him.

"Why didn't you ask me?" he said.

"About what?" his brother asked.

"About cutting off her life support."

"She died in stages, Andy. You weren't here. You weren't part of it. We didn't want to bother you." His brother filled his plate and turned away.

Andy felt a strange tingling in his head. He was back in New York, at his monthly scalp treatment with the odious collagen girl, telling her that he had changed his will, leaving everything to the church in memory of his mother. He told her how he had changed his life as well, going to church again and helping out at the soup kitchen. He even abstained from sex. When she asked if he was homosexual, he replied quickly. "Yes, but I haven't swallowed any semen." She started to laugh. Her laughter increased and was echoed by the swirling shapes around him. Andy was dizzy and disoriented. He couldn't remember where he was. Then he slowly became aware of a figure standing over him and asking something.

"Who are your next of kin? We need to know in case it's necessary to notify them." He struggled to match the words to the moving lips. What a strange question to ask, he thought. He stared up at the nurse without answering her.

On the first day after his surgery Andy felt naked without his wig, his scalp exposed, so he persuaded the nurses to let him wear a surgeon's cap. He called his friends to tell them they could come and visit him. That evening, when they came, he could tell by the intensity of their gazes that his condition was not good. They joked about the surgeon's cap. They asked him if he liked the food. Then, remembering the likely cause of his condition, they apologized for asking. When they left, the shades were drawn and the room turned gray. Hours passed and the room slowly darkened. Andy realized that he was alone, that he had always been alone. Later he awakened in the middle of the night and vividly recalled the drug-induced dream of his surgery. He remembered the holy card from the funeral home and called the nurse to ask for his wallet. He thumbed through it until he found the card. The colors were faded now and the edges worn thin.

On the second day after the operation, he grew weaker and the pain in his stomach returned with increased intensity. He was not good at pain. He liked to be in control, not to be taken by surprise or embarrassed. Repeatedly he read the chart on the wall describing the four stages of pain. Mild, Significant, Agonizing, Unbearable. Each word was illustrated by a scowling cartoon face in a parody of the usual smiley face. Eventually the doctor who had performed the surgery came to tell him that there was an unforeseen complication.

"We're working to get rid of the infection," he said. "In the meantime, I can prescribe morphine to help you cope with the pain."

Reluctantly, Andy agreed to use the morphine pump. The first time he tried it, he squeezed too hard and immediately drifted into a deep sleep. He imagined that he saw his mother lying in the bed next to him. She stared vacantly ahead while her chest heaved with each gasping breath. Then her eyes focused on him and there was a hint of recognition followed by a painful smile. Suddenly the eyes widened in panic and she whispered "Why are you here?" He went to her and bent over the bed to hear what she was saying.

"Why are you here?"

"To be with you, and tell you that I love you," he said, and kissed her on the forehead.

She smiled again, and he took her hand in his. It was red and swollen from the injection of fluids into her body. He gently stroked her arm as he stared at the tubes and machinery behind her bed. He stood there for a long time looking at her troubled face. He wanted to say something to ease her pain but he couldn't. He wanted to yank the tubes out of her body and yell "Breathe!" but he didn't. Then he heard the awful sound. It began as an urgent raspy breath that resonated from deep within her frail body. As if inflated by some invisible pump, it swelled into a cough that left her gasping for air. He reached down to stop the spasm, to comfort her, to make her well again, but he couldn't. She was lost in a blur of images and gone.

On the third day his pain became Unbearable. He thought about death. He thought about his silk-screens of *The Last Supper*. He remembered his latest work, based on a religious pamphlet he had found in the street. It was a simple piece, like a poster. No images, just words. No colors, just black letters emblazoned on a white background. It read: *Heaven and Hell Are Just One Breath Away!* Just one breath away, he thought.

Now the pain was so intense that it came from everywhere. When he was awake he tried to focus on whatever would distract him, but nothing seemed to work. He stared at the white ceiling and the white walls. White on white. Outside the sky was white too, and the day seemed brittle, like his thoughts. Now he only wanted the pain to go away and the flickering images to stop.

He squeezed the pump more often and drifted into another dream. It was like being submerged in a heavy liquid and he swam for a while, helplessly suspended and unable to breathe. Then he began to rise up toward the sunlight above. When he emerged and opened his eyes, she was there, waiting for him. They were in the old house where he had first learned to draw, sitting cross-legged on the sunlit floor. She was holding an A&W root beer for him and reached out to take his hand. "I am so proud of you," she said.

"Where are we going?" he asked.

"To church," she replied. "To see the Madonna."

"Do you forgive me?" he asked with tears in his eyes.

"Of course I do."

He smiled and took her hand.

Snow Hill

I was only fourteen when he first painted me sitting nude in a sauna. My parents were not happy about it but they said he was a famous artist. He was well known to us because he spent so much time at the Olson farm and painted many of our neighbors. Some thought him strange, but over the years I came to trust him and look forward to his visits because he made me feel special. He called me Siri but we didn't speak much. Sitting for him was boring and tiresome. I had to think about something else while he stared intently at my naked body. That and being cold were the hardest things to endure.

Siri was my first model after Christina died. She was the youngest daughter of a nearby farmer but she became a burst of life that profoundly affected my work. I painted her for nearly ten years, transported by her physical presence, lost in a futile attempt to capture what I saw. The sensuous curve of her neck, the lovely recesses of her body, the flesh tones of her breasts, the burst of hair between her thighs. Later, I did the same with Helga and her daughter. They were my obsession but I never touched any of them. Better to imagine such a thing and let the world think what it may.

My early works have few people in them and are mostly of barren landscapes or the sea, but with them I mastered the techniques I needed for success. My favorites are of the rugged coast with massive rocks leading down to the shore, their shapes rounded by centuries of wind and rain and waves. At the water's edge spindly pines are silhouetted against a dense foggy sky in the early morning light and the nearby fields are filled with golden rod and wild grasses. Tall stately trees reach up to heaven, the narrow paths between them thick with rose hips and prickly bushes. The most striking thing about these peaceful scenes is the sea that surrounds the islands and the horizon that stretches in all directions.

Christina and Helga are the bookends of my career, which includes nearly five hundred works in over fifty years. The details and techniques are flawless. I painted every blade of grass, every pore of skin, every strand of hair with great precision and no visible brushstrokes. It took years to master such things but no one notices them anymore, or else that is all they see: surface techniques with little or no content. I can still see the determined look in Christina's eyes, her self-reliance despite a crippled body, her plain and simple features, the placid smile of resignation. She never wore make-up and cared little about her appearance. Sometimes, when I recall the Olson farm, I try to imagine her childhood there. The shingled house parched grey by the sun. The rutted road and rotting woods. Fields of burnt stalks and brown grasses. In my first watercolor sketches of their farm everything is whitewashed against a pale sky. The grey house trimmed in white with wide floor boards the color of honey. The barn is quite different, dark and earthy, filled with the crude implements of farming and fishing.

I had forgotten how meager their existence was when we first met. When I look at the paintings now, I realize that we were worlds apart. They were poor and living mostly off the land, so I sketched them while they worked, he in the fields or the barn, she in the kitchen or pantry. They trusted me and tolerated my presence. I did many sketches, preliminary studies for works in tempera or oil. I tried to capture the simplicity of their lives, the colors and textures of their everyday routines. Only later did I realize that I was using them without offering any compensation.

The first sketch I did for the famous painting was made directly on the wallpaper in an upstairs bedroom. I had gone there to paint a view of the barn in the distance but was shocked when I looked out the window and saw Christina dragging herself through the field like a crab along the beach. I had no paper so I sketched her quickly on the wall, not thinking of what they might say. Because I depicted her with her back turned, most people think the woman crawling along the ground is young and attractive. But as the early watercolors show, she was middle-aged and homely. I didn't expect much response when I sent the painting off to a gallery in New York and was shocked that the Museum of Modern Art wanted to buy it. When they asked to see my early sketches, I didn't hesitate to show them. Only by seeing the preliminary studies can you appreciate the final work.

The last time I painted Christina was just a few months before she died. Later I did the same with my neighbor Karl as he lay dying, pale, and shriveled like a corpse on the bed. Then, on a whim, I painted his body outside in an imaginary snow bank. White on white in the winter landscape. Helga was a German refugee like Karl, and I first painted her in an upstairs room of his house. Like Siri, I sketched or painted her in many different poses over a period of ten years. Helga standing on a rock. Helga leaning against a tree. Helga in her great coat. Helga naked on the bed with golden highlights in her hair and subtle shadows on her body. Some of the titles I gave these works were erotic. *From the Back, Letting Her Hair Down, On Her Knees, Overflow, Crown of Flowers.* My favorite is *Overflow* in which Helga lies on her side partially covered with a thin sheet that reveals her pubic area. Moonlight from an open window falls across her breasts. Her eyes are closed, and she seems to be smiling. When I first showed it to the public, some critics said it was voyeuristic.

One day I asked Helga if I could paint her young daughter. A child with unruly hair, the girl often dressed in jeans and sneakers like a boy. In the evenings I played games with the family around their kitchen table. Dominoes or silly card games that made us laugh. When she got older, I tried not to stare at the fine hair on the back of the girl's neck, the mole on her cheek, and her long slender fingers. I admired her slim teenage figure and budding breasts clearly visible beneath a white T-shirt. I wondered what her world was like, what adolescent dreams she harbored or imagined. These were the silent secret pleasures that fed my dreams. When I first asked to paint her, Helga laughed and said, "Whatever for?" But I was pleased when she relented and allowed me to sketch the girl as she worked, helping her father in the barn or her mother in the house. Sometimes she would look at me and smile, then brush the hair from her eyes before returning to work. She reminded me of Siri and I tried to capture her delicate gestures and movements, her gleaming eyes and innocent expression. *God is in those details*, I thought as I worked. *Or else the devil.*

One night, after dinner, I showed them the finished portrait. It depicted the girl leaning against a wooden fence and gazing at the fields, her long hair ruffled by an invisible breeze. It was a study in black, white, and grey, with shadows of muted browns and greens, but the obvious focal point was the shapely figure of a beautiful young woman. She was embarrassed when she saw it and her parents were shocked. In the awkward moments that followed they rose from the table and busied themselves in the kitchen. My gaze went to the young model, who surprised me by touching my arm and saying, "It's beautiful. How can I ever thank you?" At that moment I was transfixed by her gaze, more so than by any single detail I ever painted. Later, in my nightly fantasy, I crossed the hallway that separated her bedroom from mine and silently opened the door to watch her sleep. When I came down to breakfast the next morning, the kitchen was empty. Coffee was made and freshly baked muffins were set out on the table, but there was no one in sight. I ate in silence until I heard the floorboards creak behind me and turned to see Helga standing there with a mug of coffee in her hand. "I know what you're doing," she said in a low voice. "And I want you to leave." Her steely gaze froze my impulse to speak or explain. There was no point in arguing, so I packed my things and left.

The largest but least known of my paintings is of a familiar sight near my house, a place that I have known and loved since childhood. It took nearly two years to complete, and shows six people holding hands as they dance in a circle on a snow covered hilltop. Behind them the white valley recedes toward the horizon and a pale sky stretches tightly overhead. In the distance there is a glimpse of the railroad tracks where my father and nephew were killed years ago in a tragic accident. I called the painting *Snow Hill*, which is a phrase used in "Moby Dick" to describe the hump back of the great white whale. I have read it many times and often think of myself as Ahab pursuing his obsession. I painted it as a tribute to the people I have known and used as models over the years, in gratitude for their tedious days and weeks of sitting for me. Karl and his wife are there. So is Helga, along with my friends, Allan and William. I wanted to show them all together and happy in a landscape of my own creation. Despite the winter setting they are dancing around a Maypole, each one connected to it by brightly colored ribbons. It's a joyful celebration and I dressed them up and moved them about to suit my purpose. The Maypole is intended to be phallic and there are seven ribbons but only six people. Some think the missing figure is Christina, but it's actually me waiting to die and everyone is dancing in anticipation of my death. After it was finished I added the words *Self-Portrait* to the title. With this work, I demonstrated again my mastery of technique. The scene is a monochromatic surface of subtle whites highlighted by soft greys and faded browns. I wanted to include elements of light and darkness, joy and sadness, good and evil. It's about the spiritual and the sublime in all of us, but at the same time it's very physical and visceral.

I wrestled for years with my desire for fame and the frustration of being judged so harshly by the critics. They called me an illustrator and doted on the works of that silver haired freak whose work is popular these days because his subjects are everywhere. Brillo boxes and Campbell soup cans, Elvis and Jackie, Mao and Marilyn Monroe. He is an illustrator posing as an artist. Several critics compared me to my father, to Winslow Homer and Edward Hopper, but I am better than all of them. I painted portraits of Eisenhower and Nixon in the White House. My work has hung in the Metropolitan Museum and the National Gallery of Art. I was even on the cover of *Time Magazine*. All that fuss about the Helga paintings only added to my fame, as I knew it would. For centuries great artists have used their models as a muse or mistress and no one thought anything of it. I admit now that my obsession with the erotic was subconscious, some primal urge that I could never quite satisfy. The great white whale lives in all of us.

He only painted me once, outdoors and fully clothed, but he did many sketches of me working in the house. He said I looked like a younger version of my mother, Helga, only without her smile. I took that as a compliment but when he asked me to sit for him again, she said no. I was glad because I don't have her patience. The last time I saw him he was packing up his things to leave. I hope it wasn't because of me. I tried to please him as best I could. Years later, when his paintings of her were hung in the National Gallery, mother said he was famous and she was pleased to have been his model. Me, too.

Waiting for Will

A One-Act Play

TIME AND SETTING: An indeterminate time and place

CHARACTERS: Sam: late sixties, ruggedly handsome, with long gray hair and a craggy face, he is dressed in slacks and a turtleneck

Will: late forties, slightly bald, with a moustache and goatee, he wears tights and a doublet

Helen: early thirties, strikingly beautiful, she is clad in a diaphanous gown

The lights come up to reveal a large white triangle set in the midst of a black void with a chair at each corner of the triangle. Helen sits on the upstage chair and gazes at a hand held mirror. Sam sits in the chair down left and holds a thick book in one hand as he stares into space, brooding. The chair down right is empty. A heavy metallic door slams shut and Will is thrown backwards onto the stage toward the empty chair. Sam turns to look at him.

SAM: Bravo! A breech birth!

WILL: Bloody hell! A man is born but once. *He gets up, brushes himself off, and looks at Sam.* What are you staring at?

SAM: Just trying to deduce from your clothes where you're from.

WILL: London, if you must know, but I grew up in a small town in Warwickshire. And you?

SAM: I'm a Frenchman now, though I came from Ireland.

WILL: Both hated equally by my countrymen. Why did you leave Ireland for France?

SAM: Wouldn't you, with all that dreary weather and Catholic guilt?

WILL: *He considers this.* Right. My name is Will.

SAM: I'm Sam.

WILL: *He gestures toward Helen.* And who might that be?

SAM: I've no idea.

WILL: Does she ever speak?

SAM: She did once, long ago, but it was Greek to me. *Helen stares at her reflection.* All she does is look at her mirror and primp.

WILL: *He nods.* Holding the mirror up to nature. *He looks around.* What is this place?

SAM: The dark, backward abyss of time.

WILL: *He considers this.* Right. How long have you been here?

SAM: It seems like eons, with no end in sight. You might as well get used to it. We're going to be here for a very long time. Apparently I was wrong.

WILL: About what?

SAM: Waiting. It's much worse than I thought.

WILL: What or whom are we waiting for? God?

SAM: No, his substitute.

WILL: I don't understand.

SAM: Neither do I.

WILL: *He gazes at Helen, who smiles at him.* What about her? Pleasure could make the hours seem short.

SAM: Even that would get boring after a while.

WILL: We could pretend she's Cleopatra.

SAM: *He puts down his book.* I hadn't thought of that.

WILL: *He pulls something from his doublet.* What are you reading?

SAM: I've no idea. I can't read without my spectacles. What's that in your hand?

WILL: A pen. I always carry a pen to make notes on what I see and hear. *He searches in his pockets.* But I have no ink or paper. *He gives up and gazes longingly at Helen.* Age cannot wither her nor custom stale her infinite variety.

SAM: *Recognizing the quote.* Where did you say you were born?

WILL: A small town no one's heard of called Stratford-Upon-Avon.

SAM: The glove maker's son? Things just got much more interesting! *He gets up and approaches Will.* May I ask you something?

WILL: Ask away. It seems I've nowhere else to go.

SAM: How did you...? *He pauses.* Did you really...? *He shrugs.* I don't know where to begin.

WILL: Nor do I. It's never easy but I often have help.

SAM: What do you mean?

WILL: How else could I write about kings and queens and places I've never been? I've rarely travelled farther than London and never moved in royal circles. Are you a playwright?

SAM: *He nods.* I once tried writing a play like this, but someone else beat me to it.

WILL: Like *this*? *He laughs.* If this were played upon a stage, I would condemn it as improbable fiction. There's no plot. No love or poetry or spectacle. No murders or madness!

SAM: You're right. I learned too late that no one wants gloom and doom.

WILL: What you really need are things like incest, mistaken identity, and cross-dressing.

Hearing this, Helen rises from her chair, rearranges her clothing and glances at Will, who smiles at her.

SAM: She seems to have taken an interest in you.

WILL: And I in her. Whoever loved that loved not at first sight? Her beauty is unsurpassed, beyond imagining.

SAM: *He nods.* Like a goddess.

HELEN: *She glares at them.* I am not one of those spiteful immortals! *Looking into her mirror.* Though I was once judged to be more beautiful than Aphrodite herself.

WILL: *He looks at Sam.* Could she possibly be…?

SAM: The one that Homer and other poets wrote about?

HELEN: *She comes toward them.* Those babbling twits! All they do is shout their verses while everyone around the campfire howls approval, too stupid or too drunk to understand any of it. Their tales are all lies. *Pause.* Except, of course, the ones about my beauty.

WILL: It's fortunate that you have a looking glass.

She shows them the mirror holder which has no looking glass.

SAM: How interesting. I have no spectacles to read with. You have no paper to write on. And she has no glass in the mirror to admire her beauty. It must be part of the plan.

WILL: What plan?

SAM: Fate. Fortune. Life's cruel joke. Whatever you want to call it.

HELEN: The gods fucking with us again!

WILL: Indeed. As flies to wanton boys are we to the gods. They kill us for their sport.

SAM: *To Will.* And why were you the last to arrive? You should have come after her and before me. Perhaps Einstein was right. Time is not a continuum but is curved in upon itself, like space. I'll have to rethink the whole notion of what happens after death. *He returns to his seat and broods.*

WILL: *Trying to impress Helen.* A man can die but once. Like the waves that rush toward the pebbled shore, so our minutes hasten to their end.

SAM: Will you stop with the quotes while I'm trying to think!

HELEN: *She looks at Sam and smirks.* Touchy, isn't he?

SAM: She couldn't possibly know about Homer because he came much later.

WILL: *He shrugs.* On this great stage of fools there's a blind poet in every age.

HELEN: You're right. But where I come from poets and scribes are servants who know their place. If they don't, we blind them or cut off their balls.

WILL: *Grabbing his crotch.* Ouch!

SAM: Sounds like the Ireland where I spent my youth listening to darkness, silence, and the dead.

WILL: Methinks you are too much given to brooding and melancholy.

SAM: Perhaps life is an illusion and when we look into the void afterwards we see only nothingness.

WILL: *With sudden awareness.* Is that where we are? Is this the be all and end all, the consummation devoutly to be wished for?

SAM: I'm afraid so.

WILL: But I have immortal longings in me and we can escape from this dreary place. I know we can. I feel it in my heart. *To*

Helen. Will you come with me?

HELEN: No thanks. I've had enough of sailing across the wine dark sea. It makes me sick to my stomach.

WILL: *To Sam.* What about you?

SAM: You're dreaming. There is no exit from the abyss.

WILL: But we are such stuff as dreams are made of.

SAM: No, we are a speck of dust condemned to know we are a speck of dust.

WILL: *Excited.* I will dare what others fear! *He gestures from one to the other.* I wish you well. Love all. Trust few. Do wrong to none. And so I take my leave. (He runs off stage right as the other two stare after him in silence. *After a moment he returns.* I pray you know me when we meet again. *He rushes off.*

HELEN: What a strange fellow. *She returns to her chair.*

SAM: Yes. There was much I still wanted to ask him.

HELEN: Why don't you go after him?

SAM: Because he can't escape. And because he may not be who or what he claims to be.

HELEN: *She looks into the mirror.* None of us are. But if you're right, he'll be back.

SAM: *He nods.* They always come back. *He sits in his chair and tries to read the book but quickly gives up.* If I was wrong about death and the end of consciousness, I wonder what else I was wrong about? *He looks around the stage and then at the audience.* What are we really waiting for?

A heavy metallic door slams shut and Will is thrown back-wards onto the stage toward the empty chair.

HELEN: Time to begin again. *She lowers the mirror and glares at Sam.* Speak to him.

Sam turns to face Will as the lights fade to black.

A Leaf Falls

Kevin sat alone in the dappled sunlight beneath a towering oak tree surrounded by gravestones. He gazed fondly at the sculpture of a young woman stricken with grief. Death, like love, obsessed him. The noonday sun etched deep shadows in the mourning bronze figure that knelt on one knee with her head bowed. Despite being covered with the patina of age, it was lovely in its depiction of sadness. The folds of clothing clinging to her limbs were reminiscent of Greek sculpture and the long hair falling over her shoulders reminded Kevin of Nicole. Everything reminded him of Nicole lately.

Green Mount Cemetery had once been the favorite burial site of wealthy citizens when it was on the outskirts of Baltimore but it was now surrounded by slums. He was there to write a magazine article about Hans Schuler, the sculptor of the bronze figure. At a recent class reunion a fellow graduate of Johns Hopkins said they had deluded themselves about finding jobs after college. "There are a lot of writing majors out there, churning out copy for ad agencies or trade publications" he said. Before they parted he promised that he would recommend Kevin to the editor of a local magazine. To his surprise, the editor called the following week to offer him the freelance assignment on Schuler. If the article was published, he hoped it would lead to other work. He reached into his backpack for a notebook with the introduction he had written.

Hans Schuler came to America from Germany in the last decade of the nineteenth century to study at the Rinehart School of Sculpture at the Maryland Institute College of Art. He returned to Europe briefly at the beginning of the twentieth century and won the Salon Gold Medal in Paris, the first American sculptor to do so. After returning to Baltimore, Schuler taught at the Rinehart School where he had studied and then served as director of the Maryland Institute for twenty-five years. He also opened his own studio not far away. By 1951 his traditional methods and styles were out of favor and he was asked to resign but continued to work on numerous commissions for public and private works, especially funeral monuments.

Kevin learned in his research that Hans Schuler had created the bronze grouping which graced the entrance to the Johns Hopkins campus on North Charles Street. Like countless others before him, Kevin had once rubbed the nude female figure seated at the base for good luck. Her breasts were polished to a high sheen from being touched by so many students. Schuler also created the larger-than-life size statue of Martin Luther on Thirty-Third Street and the bronze relief of General Pulaski in Patterson Park. His work could be found on the facades of public buildings as well as in parks, churches, and cemeteries all over Baltimore. Few people know about the sculptor today, even in the city where he was once famous. His style is considered a throwback to nineteenth century Romanticism, especially his depiction of sorrow and grief. The inner sadness and longing Schuler captured in his works mirrored Kevin's feelings for Nicole. They had reached the point where they would either move in together or else break up and he couldn't imagine not being with her.

They met while taking an elective course in art history during her junior year. He sat next to her and noticed how her long thin fingers traced the edge of the desk whenever she got bored in class and was smitten by her quick smile and expressive eyes. When he finally got up the nerve to speak to her, he discovered that she was a music major at the Peabody Conservatory and used those lovely long fingers to play the violin. The next day he ran into her leaving the library and they walked across campus together. "What's your favorite class this semester?" he asked.

She smiled. "History of Western Music. And you?"

"Romantic Lit" he said and told her how unrequited love was a recurring theme of nineteenth century writers. How Shakespeare's *Romeo and Juliet* was popular with the Romantics because their love was doomed to failure. But he didn't tell her that whenever he read about such things lately he thought of her.

For their first date, Nicole invited him to a concert at Shriver Hall. Kevin enjoyed it even though classical music was a mystery to him. He had never learned to read music and couldn't tell the difference between a major key and a minor key, except that one sounded happy and the other sad. One of Nicole's friends invited them to a party afterwards. Kevin wasn't fond of parties but agreed to go. The tiny apartment was filled with mostly music majors. He felt uncomfortable listening to their conversation about intervals and octaves and decided that musicians must hear things in their heads that only they can hear. He wondered what Nicole heard when she played the violin. Were the chords and melodic structure a physical, sensual experience, or totally abstract? Did she hear them in her sleep and when she made love?

On their second date, she took him to a performance at a grungy place on North Avenue that combined a bar, art gallery, and small stage in a long narrow room. A group of young musicians played the spaced out melodies of Philip Glass while video images of disconnected people and places were projected on the walls. When it was over Nicole said, "That was totally awesome." Kevin nodded even though he didn't really understand it. They dated for the next six months, and he decided to stay in Baltimore after graduation to try freelance writing for a year while she finished school.

After his trip to Green Mount Cemetery, he texted Nicole and asked her to meet him at the Starbucks in Charles Village. They ordered lattes and sat across from each other at a table by the window. He told her what he had learned about Schuler's bronze figures in his research for the article. "They're cast in a foundry," he said, "just like a steel mill. Then they're fired in clay or sand and hammered into shape. That's why they can last forever." He looked into Nicole's eyes and said, "I think the female mourning figures are very moving."

She smiled. "I'm glad you're writing again. I was afraid you'd given up."

Kevin was surprised by the comment but didn't say anything. Instead he took a deep breath and decided to ask about their living arrangements. "So, when can we move in together?"

Her smile disappeared and she shook her head. "Not yet, Kevin."

"But we've been dating for almost a year now. Aren't you happy?"

"Yes, but I'm not ready for that."

"There're only a few months left before you graduate. What happens then?"

"I have to get past my senior recital before I can think about that. I'm practicing day and night." She paused before adding, "Besides, you're very self-sufficient. You like being alone, but I need to be around people."

Kevin's heart sank. It always came down to this. He was quiet and introspective, unsure of his abilities, while she was outgoing, popular, and self-confident. "You have lots of friends," he said. "They're just not mine." When she didn't respond, he reached out and touched her hand. "Nicole, I love you and I want to be with you."

She lowered her eyes and stared at her coffee cup. "You're grasping and you know how I feel about that." She had recently found Zen, or at least her version of it, and believed the most meaningful life was not filled with grasping or self-gratification but a peaceful openness to whatever might happen. Unfortunately for Kevin, that also meant indifference to emotional and physical attachments. The last time they spent the night together, she seemed distracted. When he asked if she'd enjoyed making love, she was silent at first. "Yes," she finally said before rising from the bed. "But I need to practice now." He realized she was obsessed with music even before she started to practice for the recital. Maybe that's why she was so good at it.

Kevin went back to work on the article but wondered if he would ever be as good at writing as Nicole was at playing the violin. He had reached the mid-point of his work when he made an interesting discovery about the relationship between music and writing.

Schuler designed the Sidney Lanier Memorial at the entrance to the Johns Hopkins campus. The nineteenth century poet is seated on a boulder with a pad and pencil in hand as, if writing or composing, and a flute lies on the rock beside him. Lanier was a flute player for the Peabody Conservatory Orchestra as well as a poet who lectured at Hopkins. His unique style of poetry was based on a theory connecting poetic meter with musical notation.

During his next visit to Green Mount Cemetery Kevin made detailed notes on the gravestone figures by Schuler. Women bent over with grief, their heads shrouded. Men praying over the tombs of their loved ones. Angels gazing toward heaven with their hands on their hearts. The artist had depicted their responses to death as sad rather than hopeful, human rather than divine, as if heartbreak and loneliness were too much to bear despite the promise of salvation. Kevin spent hours studying them and was reluctant to leave.

When he met Nicole for lunch the day before her recital, he was still working on the final draft of his article. She insisted on going to the One World Café on University Boulevard. "I love it here," she said after they ordered. "It's Vegan, Zen, and Organic. Food for your body, your soul, and your conscience." She smiled and looked at him with her dark brown eyes. He was enchanted by her smile and those expressive eyes. The hair falling over her shoulders reminded him of Schuler's bronze reliefs. When the waitress brought their drinks, Nicole took a sip of her tea and said, "Did you go to the cemetery this morning?"

He nodded. "I went at sunrise. It's beautiful there in the early morning light and I thought of you." He thought of her all the time now, especially since she told him she was thinking of moving back to New York after graduation and applying to Julliard.

"You're such a Romantic," she said and looked away. "Did I ever tell you that I joined the choir of a Catholic church in high school? Not because I believed or anything like that, but because I wanted to learn Gregorian chant. It's different because every note is sung with equal duration and emphasis. It's a perfect fusion of words and music, restrained but expressive."

Kevin was puzzled. "How can it be restrained and expressive at the same time? And why are you telling me this?"

She turned to look at him. "Isn't that what writing is all about?" Then she surprised him by saying, "Isn't that what you said Schuler did with his sculpture?" She was right but Kevin frowned and said nothing. They sat in silence until the waitress brought their food. Nicole looked at the portabella mushroom burger with dismay and began to dissect it, carefully removing bits of onion with her fingers. "I should have told her no onions," she said. Then, ignoring the food, she sighed and looked at Kevin. "I've been thinking that maybe you should see someone."

He nearly choked on his grilled chicken sandwich before he could answer. "I *am* seeing someone. You."

"I mean a doctor. Someone who could help with your sadness and obsession with death."

He was stunned. "You think I have an obsession with death because I spend so much time at the cemetery?"

She poked at the stringy tentacles of onion on her plate. "Yes."

"But it's part of my research."

She sighed. "We are so different, Kevin. You're an introvert and I'm the exact opposite. That makes it hard on both of us." He watched her bite into the mushroom burger while he tried to digest the meaning of what she said. No one had ever called him an introvert before. Shy, maybe, or quiet, but not an introvert. She swallowed and said, "Besides, you want to settle here and I hate this city. My teachers won't even send their kids to the schools here." Kevin knew that one of her classmates had been stabbed while waiting for the commuter bus from Peabody to the main campus. The girl survived but Nicole was so shaken that she never forgot, even though it happened almost a year ago. When she spoke again, her tone was more serious. "I've said before that nothing is cast in stone between us."

He smirked. "Or in bronze, either." He stared at her and then said, "Maybe we should have used the lost wax method instead of sand." He said this to hurt her but also to see if she remembered what he had told her about bronze casting.

She ignored his sarcasm and talked instead about her senior recital, a Mozart sonata for violin and piano that required total coordination between both performers. "It's a very demanding piece," she said. "I'm meeting Justin this afternoon to practice, so I'll be busy for the rest of the day."

Kevin took the bus downtown after lunch. He enjoyed exploring the architecture of the city and browsing the second hand shops in the old neighborhoods. He usually went alone now that Nicole was practicing so much, but that didn't bother him. When the bus passed Peabody Conservatory, he thought about how being in love had its own kind of sadness, especially if you loved someone more than they loved you. He got off the bus at Fells Point, walked to the end of the pier, and stared at the water. It reminded him of the ending he had written for the article.

Schuler's masterpiece, which he proposed at the end of his career, was a colossal version of The Four Horsemen of the Apocalypse. He intended it for a sight overlooking the harbor but the city fathers rejected the work because of the immense size and cost. It survives only in a small plaster model which his family is fond of showing visitors to their studio.

The next morning Kevin read over the final draft. He was late meeting the deadline and thought it probably wouldn't get published, but he submitted it anyhow. After he hit the send button on his computer he realized that writing about another person's life was like being in love with someone who was totally different than you. He knew Nicole's taste in food and music. He knew about her intense dedication to practice and performing. He even knew about the tattoo on her lower back and the birthmark on her inner thigh, but he didn't really know her. Despite extensive research and interviews with Schuler's surviving family, despite studying his work and poring over old photographs, he hadn't really learned what Hans Schuler was like as a person. Did he enjoy working in solitude? Was he sculpting his own feelings about death when he created those beautiful mourning figures? Was he discouraged when his proposal for the *Four Horsemen* was rejected by the city?

That evening, as he walked through the lobby of the Peabody Library on his way to Nicole's recital, Kevin noticed two pedestals flanking the entrance and recognized the bust on one even before he saw the name on the base. He was thrilled to see the bronze head of Sidney Lanier by Hans Schuler at the Peabody because Lanier had found a connection between music and literature in his theory of poetic meter. He couldn't find the artist's name inscribed on the back, but his heart soared because it seemed an unexpected and hopeful link between Nicole's music and his own writing.

The small auditorium was filled with faculty and students when he entered for the recital. The lights dimmed as Nicole and Justin entered from the wings, he in a tuxedo and she in a black evening dress. Justin sat waiting at the keyboard as Nicole raised her bow. When they launched into the lively melody of the first movement, Kevin was surprised by the expressiveness of her playing. Her eyebrows arched and her head nodded with the rhythm. She seemed to be leading Justin not only in tempo but in energy and passion. As he gazed at her bare shoulders and sensuous neck, Kevin was entranced by her beauty and the sound of Mozart's music. Despite their differences, he realized that he loved her more than ever. He wanted desperately to share her thoughts and feelings, to spend the rest of his life with her. Most of all he wanted her to love him as much as he loved her.

The second movement was much slower, but Nicole's concentration was just as intense and Justin responded to her every move. Kevin had heard her practice the piece many times without the piano accompaniment. Now he saw what he had only sensed before: how both performers heard the same thing in their heads and spoke to each other with their instruments, something he could never do. The sense of hope and connection he felt earlier vanished and his heart sank. During the final movement he couldn't bear to look at the stage. Instead he stared at his knees, the tips of his shoes, at the seat back in front of him. As the sweet sadness of the melody seeped into his consciousness, he felt the keen disappointment of unrequited love. How could music be so beautiful and sad at the same time? At the end of the performance, he slowly got to his feet and joined the rest of the audience in a standing ovation.

Nicole had promised there would be time after her recital to discuss their future, but he knew that wasn't necessary. She and Justin would be invited to a party by their friends to celebrate and they might even go home together. There was no point in waiting around. As he left the building, Kevin stopped at the bust of Sidney Lanier and searched again behind the bronze head until he found the artist's name. It wasn't Hans Schuler after all but a sculptor he had never heard of.

When he got back to his apartment, there was an e-mail from the magazine editor asking him to meet a photographer at the cemetery for a photo shoot of Schuler's works. The editor wanted him to explain in greater detail how the sculptures were examples of Romanticism but no other changes were necessary. Kevin was elated. He wanted to text Nicole and share the good news but thought better of it when he imagined her spending the night with Justin. He worked on the changes until two in the morning. When he finished, his heartbreak was tempered by a new sense of purpose. He would stay in Baltimore after Nicole went back to New York and continue to write.

His article was finally published around the time she started at Julliard. He celebrated by visiting Green Mount Cemetery one last time. The leaves were just beginning to fall as he sat under the same towering oak and gazed at the familiar bronze sculpture. When a leaf fell to the ground in front of him, he thought of his favorite poem by EE Cummings. It consisted of a single word, loneliness, spelled vertically as *l(one) liness.* Beneath it the poet added the tag *a leaf falls.* Kevin loved how the image of a falling leaf mirrored the meaning and spiral of the word. No matter how much you love someone, there's always a part of you that still feels lonely. He knew that he would eventually get over Nicole despite the intensity of his feelings, but he still thought of her whenever he heard a violin sonata or saw one of Schuler's mourning figures.

Gods and Warriors

While scuba diving one day I found something buried at the bottom of the sea. First I saw a hand and an arm. Then I uncovered the rest of the body. — Stefano Mariottini, August 1972

The trip to Calabria took longer than expected. Stefano and his friend Mikael took a high-speed train from Rome to Naples but then had to board a slow train that only made one trip a day with lots of stops along the way. They stared out the window to relieve their boredom as the train passed factories, warehouses, and a power plant with its smokestacks reaching toward the heavens. Then the peaceful countryside came into view with cows and sheep and a distant view of hills. They were both avid scuba divers and passed the time by talking about their plans for the week. They had booked a cheap hotel in Riace, a small town on the Ionian coast where they planned on hiring a boat to reach the diving sites they wanted to explore. As the train pulled into the station Mikael said, "This whole area is called Magna Graecia because of the Greek ruins. I'd like to check them out while we're here." Stefano nodded in agreement. As a teenager he had gone to Sicily with his grandfather and seen Greek ruins there. He admired their symmetry and balance as well as the repetition of classical details. Later, at university, he wanted to be an architect but didn't have the drafting skills, so he decided to be a chemist instead.

The diving in Riace was incredible and so was the view of the Ionian Sea from their balcony. Stefano was amazed by the colors, shades of green that were nothing like the wine dark sea mentioned by Homer. In the evening pink and orange clouds reflected the setting sun and reminded him of a Michelangelo painting. The week went by so quickly that they almost forgot about the Greek ruins. They were a huge disappointment when they finally saw them on Thursday. The crumbled walls could have been anywhere, with no clue as to how old they might be or what they were used for. Friday was the last day of their vacation, so they left the hotel early and headed to the beach for a full day of diving. The guide they hired helped them on board his boat and headed for an area they hadn't seen yet. After exploring the sea bottom for several hours, they were ready to head back to the boat for lunch when Stefano noticed a dark shape protruding from the bottom. It looked like a man's arm and he thought for a moment it must be a dead body. After clearing away a layer of sandy mud, he saw that it was a statue of some sort and not a corpse. It was large and well preserved, so he signaled to Mikael and together they tried to pull it free from the bottom but it was too heavy. Then he noticed another figure not far away. While he worked on uncovering that one, Mikael swam back to tell the guide and get some rope.

It took an hour of hard work for them to raise the first statue to the surface and onto the boat. Then they headed to the beach and hauled it ashore. A crowd soon gathered to see what they had found and someone took a picture of them standing beside the figure. It appeared to be a god or warrior of some kind and was obviously very old. Stefano decided to notify the town officials because there were strict rules in Italy about finding items of historical interest. The local police came to check it out and they managed to pull the second one up the next day. Both statues were larger than life, almost seven feet tall, and each one weighed nearly three hundred pounds. Several reporters came to interview Stefano, who beamed with pleasure at his unexpected find.

In the weeks and months that followed, lots of so-called experts came to see the figures. Eventually they were hauled off to a university for cleaning and further study. Stefano was obsessed by who the two figures were and how they ended up at the bottom of the sea, so he continued to follow what happened in the newspapers. Their origin was eventually narrowed to around 450 BC in the south of Greece. The most likely sculptor was Polyclitus, who invented the contrapposto pose that used a mathematical formula to depict the human body in a realistic stance. The strangest thing the university people came up with was something called ascrotal symmetry, which Stefano and Mikael both joked about. Apparently, the sculptural depiction of testes changed from the earliest classical period, when both testicles were of equal size and height, to the most recent period, when the left testicle was depicted as larger and lower. The experts concluded that this characteristic is either anatomically incorrect or due to a pathological condition such as varicocele, which may have been common at the time.

A more difficult question to answer was how the two figures ended up on the bottom of the sea where they were found. Because Roman emperors greatly admired Greek sculpture, they often had them shipped to Rome for display. The most common sea route from Greece to Rome was around the southern tip of Italy and a storm or shipwreck off the coast of Calabria would have resulted in the two figures being found there. The answer to the question concerning their identity was proposed by scholars familiar with ancient Greek myths. Due to their warlike stance and similar features, a possible explanation is that they depicted the two sons of Oedipus who fought and killed each other after their father blinded himself. Their fate is chronicled in the tragedy "Seven Against Thebes" and many scholars accept this theory. Stefano had never read the play about Oedipus and was shocked by what he learned. The infamous king of Thebes never lusted after his own mother, despite what Freud and others said. As a young man, he answered a riddle about the three ages of man and was rewarded with the crown and the queen as his wife. Years later, when he learned the truth from a blind prophet, he blinded himself and went into exile. Greek scholars consider it a tale about how we are cursed by the gods with blindness to the truth.

The restoration of the bronzes took almost ten years, after which the statues were stored in a warehouse for another four years before being sent to Florence for additional study. During that time most people lost interest while Stefano continued his boring work as a chemist, married and divorced twice, and searched for excitement in scuba diving. He had hoped that after making such a startling discovery his life would change somehow, but that didn't happen. Although he never found anything as fascinating as the two bronze figures from Riace, he still believed that more figures like them may be hidden deep beneath the sea, reminders of what used to be in that part of the world.

After the experts were satisfied with their answers, a museum was finally built in Calabria to house the two statues. Stefano was rewarded for his discovery by being invited to the opening, where he briefly relived the excitement and wonder of the day he found them. He had lost contact with Mikael over the years and hoped that his friend might show up at the museum, but that didn't happen. The figures were displayed in their own gallery, mounted on separate marble platforms made to withstand tremors or earthquake. They were aston-ishing to behold in a pose that was both athletic and graceful. Each had realistic eyes with fine copper lashes. One had bared teeth made of silver and the other had holes in his hairline where a helmet was once attached. Both had the intense and threatening look typical of warriors at the time. While he was admiring them, Stefano noticed an old man closely inspecting the groin of one figure. As he reached out to touch the stat-ue's testicles, a museum guard quickly moved in to stop him. The man looked at the guard and said gruffly, "I'm the scholar who proved why his balls are like that!" Stefano laughed out loud before heading to the opening ceremony. When he was introduced as the man who found the Riace bronzes, he was reminded of his fifteen minutes of fame.

He finally retired after thirty years of filling prescriptions at the same pharmacy in Rome, but he was no longer able to scuba dive because of a heart problem. He had time then to read more about ancient Greece and to travel there. At the Acropolis Museum in Athens he discovered that the scholars and historians were right after all. The marble and stone sculpture from the classical period is inferior to the more realistic bronze statues of that time. He also saw the larger-than-life size statue of Athena dressed as a warrior ready to defend her followers. Like the two warrior figures from Riace, she is a reminder that they came from a violent and terrible world. Brother killing brother because they thought the gods wanted them to. The civilized citizens of Athens practicing enslavement and genocide to protect their privileged position.

On his way back to Rome, Stefano sailed past the coast of Calabria where he found the statues. As he watched the sun setting beyond the distant hills, he realized that many of the things he once believed weren't true anymore. The bronze statues he found aren't gods or mortal heroes after all. They're not even historical people who lived long ago, but part of the mythical family of Oedipus cursed by the gods. During the 2000 years they rested on the ocean floor, we conquered heaven and earth, but millions of lives were lost in wars or religious conflicts over what to believe. Life is full of chaos and suffering which goes on forever, and belief in gods of any kind isn't likely to change that.

Ocean State

My paintings are very graphic—or pornographic, depending on your point of view—and very explicit. A lot of skin and pubic hairs. A lot of excretions and fluids dripping down the canvas. Lips, tongues, and genitals in vivid pinks, reds, and yellows. Some have the hyper-realistic look of television commercials or video games. Others have high contrast or grainy images that overlap one another like a collage. I like to use real textures and objects, like fishnet, chain-link, steel or plastic tubes, broken glass, and torn posters from rock concerts. Looking at them makes you feel like you've eaten or drunk too much. You're fascinated but also repulsed. My goal is to arouse different reactions to the same bodily image: revulsion along with the realization that it's shockingly beautiful in its own way. It's an obsession that started when I was in high school.

*

"Feet are disgusting," Jeff said as he wiggled his misshapen toes in the sand. We were sitting on the beach, staring at the ocean, and I had to admit his toes were pretty disgusting even though the rest of his body was sexy. The tide was coming in, so we had to move before it washed over our feet. "Did you ever hear of intercrural sex?" he asked as we got up and started walking. When I shook my head he said, "It's what ancient Greek men did with their boy lovers." My heart skipped a beat. *Was he telling me he's gay?* I wanted to ask where he learned that but I didn't have to. Jeff was the smartest person I knew and if he had something on his mind, he didn't let go until he learned everything about it. He stopped suddenly, pointing at the ground. I couldn't make out what he saw at first because it was almost the same color as the sand. Then he mumbled the words *rubber sex* and I realized it was a used condom.

We grew up together in Middletown, as did lots of other kids because there's a Middletown in nearly every state. Ours was in Rhode Island, appropriately labeled *The Ocean State* on our license plates. Jeff and I became friends in first grade when he saw me peeing behind a tree near the playground and asked why I was squatting like that. When I joined the Girl Scouts at the age of eight, my mother told me that nice girls don't pee in the woods. And when I started dating, she told me nice girls don't have sex until they get married. The problem was I didn't want to be a nice girl. In our sophomore year of high school Jeff told me his penis got really big when he was aroused. After that we shared all of our discoveries about sex, even though—with one notable exception—we never did it together.

Middletown is a suburb of Newport and has two beaches that face the ocean. With their typical lack of imagination, the locals call them First Beach and Second Beach. First Beach is near the cliff walk in Newport where the mansions built by the rich are located. Between First and Second Beach is a popular landmark called the Chasm, a giant vertical cleft carved into the rocky promontory thousands of years ago by a receding glacier. The Chasm is only ten feet wide but almost a hundred feet high. Jeff said it resembled a giant vagina or else the crack of an asshole, depending on your point of view. The Chasm is a favorite hangout of local teenagers, many of whom like to have sex on the sandy floor of its dark interior. That can be tricky, though, because it's easy to get trapped inside by the rising tide. You have to get in, have your fun, and then get out before you're drenched by the salt water rushing in. In the midst of their frantic fucking some of the guys will shout, "Here it comes! Here it comes!" and they aren't just referring to the tide.

The Chasm is near the intersection where Purgatory Road meets Paradise Avenue, which Jeff and I thought was hilarious because having sex there could either be a sin or a heavenly pleasure. Another local landmark is a private boarding school called St. George's, which sits on a hilltop overlooking the ocean and its Gothic spires can be seen from miles away. The tuition is outrageously expensive and the students all come from rich families in New England. Locals can't afford it and probably wouldn't go there even if they could because it's so snobbish. My dad once applied for a teaching job at St. George's and was turned down because he wasn't a graduate of Yale or Harvard. He was a Classics teacher who named his daughter Cassandra, after the woman in Greek mythology whose prophecies were never believed. Fortunately, my mother came up with the nickname Casey, but the name Cassandra stuck—and turned out to be prophetic.

In our junior year, Jeff and I both had summer jobs at Second Beach, me at the concession stand and Jeff cleaning out the locker rooms. He delighted in telling me the obscene things he found written on the walls there, like *What's the difference between a vagina and an asshole?* I thought that was disgusting, like seeing the used condom on the beach, but Jeff said the answer depended on how drunk you were and who you were with at the time. When he finally told me that he preferred boys to girls, I wasn't totally surprised because I occasionally saw him checking out the guys on the beach.

Unlike some of our friends who liked the thrill of screwing inside the Chasm, Jeff and I had sex together for the first and only time on the grounds of St. George's. One night after working all day at the beach, we met up with some friends to drink beer in the woods behind the school library. We liked to hang out there in the summer when the campus was deserted. After consuming several six-packs, we had a rambling discussion about the word *horny* and whether or not it applied to girls. "Horny refers to satyrs," one of the guys said. "Those funny creatures with horns and tails and the legs of a goat that are always chasing after nymphs. Their horns stand for the male sex drive, so how can it apply to girls?" I was lying with my head on Jeff's lap at the time and felt him getting hard beneath me. When I sat up and stared at him, I must have looked surprised because he said, "I can do it with girls if I really want to." We had sworn there would be no sexual secrets between us, so I had a sudden urge to test him and see if he was telling the truth. I was also drunk and eager to get laid for the first time.

After the others had left I said, "Girls get horny, too, and I can prove it." Then I led him to a secluded spot beneath a large metal sculpture shaped like the figure eight. While Jeff fumbled with a condom, I lay in the grass and noticed two words scratched on the underside of the metal. The first was *Fuck*, which I expected to be followed by *you*, but I looked closer and realized it said *Fuck me*. I shouted, "Fuck me!" and to my surprise and delight, that's exactly what Jeff did.

During our senior year I noticed in art class how Jeff liked drawing nude men in strange positions, so I jokingly asked if he was a top or a bottom. When he admitted that he was a bottom, I had this image of him writhing beneath another guy with a combination of pleasure and pain. Later, on our spring field trip to the Metropolitan Museum in New York, he dragged me past dozens of vase paintings in the ancient Greek section until he found what he was looking for. "Check this out," he said, pointing to a nude male warrior with an erection. A woman was climbing on top of him and reaching for his penis. "I read that women who did that were hookers and the men actually preferred having sex with young boys."

I rolled my eyes. "But what if they weren't hookers, just strong women who knew what they wanted, like Antigone or Helen of Troy?" Jeff looked at me but said nothing. The following week, when I asked him to be my date for the senior prom, he gladly accepted. Some of our classmates thought it was shocking because he was openly gay long before it was acceptable but we thought it was hilarious and a great way to celebrate our friendship. We also knew we would have more fun together than with anyone else.

After graduation we were both fortunate to get into the

Rhode Island School of Design, also known as RISD, where we continued to share an obsession with sex. Hardly a day went by that we didn't find something erotic in our art history book. Japanese *shunga* prints that showed in graphic detail two lovers having sex beneath their kimonos. Penises on Greek and Roman statues that always looked small and uncircumcised. When Jeff saw all the fig leaves in early Renaissance art, he laughed and said, "I think we should write an illustrated history of sex and call it *Assholes and Vaginas in Famous Works of Art*. Later he showed me a nineteenth century painting by Gustav Courbet in our textbook that depicted a close-up view of a naked woman seen from the foot of a bed. Courbet called it *The Origin of the World*, which suggested to me that she was meant to be some kind of goddess or mother earth figure. When I looked closer, I saw that her face was totally hidden.

"It's beautiful," I said. "But she has no head, no face, and no identity. She's just another sex object for men to stare at."

Jeff nodded. "So why do you think he called it that?"

"Maybe because everyone comes from a womb? Or because life begins when semen enters the vagina?"

He rolled his eyes and said, "Not if you're fucking the other way."

In the late seventies, RISD wasn't as liberal as Brown— where everyone supposedly declared their sexual orientation on the first day of class—but we still had our share of outrageous behavior. There was a big controversy about body piercings by nude models in our drawing class. It started with female models who had pierced noses, lips, and eyebrows. Then male models showed up wearing studs on their foreskin and females with their nipples pierced. The most frequently asked question in class was whether or not we had to include those details in our sketches. I think the whole body piercing thing was a kind of running joke about how far we could go with studs, tattoos, and hair dyed every color in the rainbow. Today people cover their bodies with elaborate tattoos of vines, flowers, and other organic shapes. Their whole body is a work of art, and I get it, but I can't help wondering if they will still like it twenty years from now.

After our freshman year Jeff decided his interests were more scholarly than artistic, so he left RISD to study for a degree in art history at Yale. We still saw each other occasionally, because New Haven isn't that far from Providence. After that he went to Oxford University to earn a doctorate while I stayed in the Ocean State. Several years later he came back to RISD to give a lecture about the failure of abstract art to connect with people on a physical or emotional level. I was still living in Providence at the time, putting together my portfolio, so I asked him to look at my paintings. He didn't say much about them until we went to dinner afterwards.

"Your work is good," he said. "But it lacks passion. It's not really *you* because you haven't tapped into your deepest feelings." He sat back, took a sip of wine, and smiled. "I think that making or appreciating great art is like discovering sex." I was disappointed, and looked away. Jeff ordered a second bottle of wine and we talked freely about sex, just like the old days. He laughed when I recalled the time we walked along the beach and he found a used condom in the sand. I remembered that it was filled with semen on the inside and smeared with shit on the outside. I must have been feeling the effects of the wine, because I said something that I would later regret. "I've never told you this, but I think anal sex is disgusting."

Jeff rolled his eyes in disbelief. "Casey, it's time you

admitted there really is such a thing as anal orgasm caused by stimulation of the prostate from behind."

I smirked. "That's fine for you, but I don't have a prostate." Then, in full Cassandra mode, I said, "Anal sex will be the end of you someday." He glared at me and I swallowed hard, not knowing where that came from or why I said it. I mumbled an apology and added, "Maybe I'm just trying to get back at you for your frank opinion of my work."

"You shouldn't feel that way," he said. "You're really talented and I know you'll be successful once you find your own style."

Jeff's career as an art critic flourished and he travelled abroad frequently. He always sent me postcards from museums he visited that featured erotic works of art. Bouguereau's *Abduction of Psyche* from 1895 with an idealized female nude born aloft by a sexy young god. Boucher's *Leda and the Swan*, which depicted a reclining nude exposing her genitals to Zeus, who took the form of a swan that eagerly approached her with his beak. He said he had started a file of such works for the book we would someday write together. He eventually became the art critic for a national magazine based in New York, and was appointed to the board of trustees at RISD, where he lobbied for them to hire me as an artist-in-residence. By then I had a major breakthrough in my work after seeing *The Dinner Party* by Judy Chicago.

Her name wasn't really Judy Chicago. She chose it after her husband died and she became an ardent feminist. She often used the term *multi-orgasmic* when referring to her sex life, and one of her early paintings shows a large, disembodied penis flying through the air. *The Dinner Party* fills an entire room with a triangular table that has 39 place settings for mythical and historical women honored by name. Many of the images on the porcelain plates and embroidered linens are sexual in nature: flowers, butterflies, and other shapes suggestive of vulvas. After seeing *The Dinner Party*, I began work on a series of large paintings unlike anything I'd ever done before. I was living in a loft cum studio in Newark, where I taught part-time at a junior high school, and I worked furiously for a whole year until I felt ready to show my new work to someone. Not just anyone, but the one person whose opinion mattered the most.

When I invited Jeff to come see the paintings, he looked around the loft at my sparse furnishings and cluttered studio without comment. Then he spied the large canvases and went straight to them. I waited nervously as he carefully inspected each one. Finally, he said, "Casey, these are amazing. I mean, really amazing. Whatever inspired you to go in this direction?" When I told him about *The Dinner Party*, he nodded. "There was a lot of experimental art with a feminist edge in the seventies, but it died out quickly. I think now is a good time for a comeback." He sat down next to me on my sagging futon. "I know several gallery owners in the city who would love this kind of thing. Let me talk to them about showing your work. If they do, I'll write a glowing review." I was so thrilled that I hugged him and opened a bottle of cheap champagne to celebrate. We drank a toast as he looked more closely at the dried texture of dripping paint on several canvases. Then he eyed me suspiciously. "Are you sure there are no real excretions on these works?"

I laughed and said, "Believe me, I was sorely tempted."

The gallery show in New York later that year was a huge success. Before it opened, Jeff said that I should sign the new paintings *Cassandra O*. I had signed my previous work Casey

Olsen but I liked his suggestion because I sensed that this was the beginning of something new and important in my career, something that came from deep inside me. Jeff was right about that, just as he was about so many other things.

On his subsequent travels abroad, he continued to send me examples of art that depicted explicit sex, insisting they were for our intended book. They included a picture from the British Museum of Japanese prints that showed Buddhist monks sodomizing young recruits, a postcard from Greece of an ancient stone marker with an erect phallus pointing up at the head of the god Hermes, and a postcard from Germany of Ernst Kushner's pre-pubescent nude with an inverted black triangle between her legs. But after several years of doing this, he suddenly stopped. There was a period of about six months or so when I didn't hear from him at all.

I knew that lots of young men were dying from something called the gay cancer, so when he wrote and told me about his illness, I was devastated—especially after my unintended prophecy to him that night at dinner. In his letter he asked me to record a playlist, a collection of his favorite music that he could listen to while on the morphine he took to ease his pain. He listed songs by Leonard Cohen and Bruce Springsteen, but also classical works by Beethoven and Mozart and something called *Spiegel im Spiegel* by a contemporary composer named Arvo Part.

When I took the tape to him in New York, he was already bedridden and attended by a visiting nurse. Shocked by his appearance, I fought back tears and put my hand on his wrist that was so thin I could have circled it with two fingers. He put his other hand on mine and said, "Thanks for the playlist. My favorite is the piece by Arvo Part. The slow repetition of solitary notes reminds me of the friends I've lost, but it leaves me feeling peaceful." The he smiled weakly. "It's probably the closest I'll ever get to heaven."

I'd never heard Jeff describe his feelings that way. I swallowed hard and said, "What happened? You always told me you never had unprotected sex."

He sighed and looked away. "The last time I was in London I met a young man from South Africa who spoke with a lovely Oxford accent. We spent the night together, but neither of us had a condom and we couldn't stop ourselves. I never saw him again and noticed the first symptoms not long after that." He looked directly at me. "I want to be cremated, Casey, and I need you to help make the arrangements. There's no one else I can count on." Before I could reply, he said, "And I expect you to finish that book without me. The rough draft and all my notes are packed up in a box here in the living room."

He lasted barely a month after my visit. I arranged for the cremation and was able to see him again the day before he died. I was fortunate to be with him then, but I'm glad his suffering is over. I keep the urn with his ashes in my studio where I sometimes listen to the piece by Arvo Part. The two melodies on the piano and cello seem to mirror each other. Whenever I hear it, I'm reminded of how much Jeff meant to me, how he was brave enough and outrageous enough to be himself no matter what other people might think or say.

I finished the book a year after his death and dedicated it to him. I was tempted to write "To my dearest friend, who knew the difference between a vagina and an asshole." But I knew the editors wouldn't allow that, so I called it *Love and Lust in Erotic Art*. With the money I hope to get from the book, I'm planning a gallery show called *Dicks* that will feature paintings and sculpture by women artists which represent the male power structure throughout history. It's intended to be very satirical and a former student of mine wants to include fake plaster casts of penises from Henry VIII and Sigmund Freud. It's been almost twenty years since I first saw *The Dinner Party*, which is now enshrined at the Brooklyn Museum of Art. Most of the old taboos are gone against women, blacks, and gays, but who's to say they won't come back to haunt us again? Life, like art, is often cyclical.

*

That's how my work became what some consider disgusting or degenerate. I live in New York now, but occasionally go back to Middletown. I walk along Second Beach past the overweight old people, weary middle aged parents, indifferent college students, and little kids playing happily in the surf. I look out at the horizon and remember thinking in high school that the ocean was the closest thing to infinity I could imagine. How it's always the same yet always changing. The tide is going out or else coming in, but it's hard to tell which unless you're in the Chasm. That dark mysterious cleft in the rock is like a giant womb, someplace we all came from and long to return to. It's a metaphor for something Jeff and I came to understand before he died. It represents the origin of the world and what happens when we eventually die and fertilize the earth. Life is a continuous dance of love and death, Eros and Thanatos. Even Freud knew that, and he was a real asshole.

Rapture

One-Act Play

TIME: The near future

SETTING: The upper floor of a high rise apartment building in
  Philadelphia

CHARACTERS:

Eric: Late forties, academic type, a bit reserved

Josh: College age, bright and eager, but somewhat naïve

Orlando: Early sixties, sophisticated and overly dramatic

*The lights come up on a small living room with clothes and
boxes strewn about on the floor. Eric is seated on a couch stage
left staring at a large picture on the opposite wall. Startled by
a loud knocking, he gets up quickly and goes to the front door.*

ERIC: Who's there? *After a muffled reply, he unlocks and opens the door.*

Oh my God! You look awful. Are you alright? *He steps aside and gestures at the sofa.* Come in. Have a seat.

JOSH: Thanks. *He goes to the sofa and sits, clutching a small black book in his hands.*

ERIC: It's getting dangerous out there and I really wasn't expecting anyone.

JOSH: Not even God's messenger in the final days? I'm here to save you from sin and damnation.

ERIC: I don't believe in God. *He sits on the sofa.* But I am afraid of going to hell.

JOSH: Then you will accept Jesus as your Lord and Savior?

ERIC: Absolutely not.

JOSH: *He holds up the small black book.* But it is written that you will burn in everlasting flames for resisting His saving grace.

ERIC: I think there are many ways to find what you mean by salvation. *Pause.* Are you thirsty? I'm afraid all I have is water.

JOSH: No, thanks, I'm fine. Just a little tired.

ERIC: What's it like out there in the streets?

JOSH: Getting worse. There are a lot of people wearing camouflage and carrying assault rifles.

ERIC: That would be the National Guard enforcing martial law. *He pauses.* What's your name?

JOSH: I'm called Josh.

ERIC: Joshua? How appropriate. That's very biblical.

JOSH: *He shrugs.* Not really. When my mom told my dad she was pregnant, he said you must be joshing and the name kind of stuck. But I believe in what the bible says. *He opens the black book and reads aloud.* 'For the Lord Himself will descend from heaven with the voice of an archangel and the sound of a trumpet. Then we who remain shall be caught up together in the clouds to meet the Lord.'

ERIC: You left out something very important. 'And the dead in Christ shall rise first.' According to Saint Paul, the Last Judgment comes before the Rapture.

JOSH: *Surprised.* You've read Scripture and you still don't believe?

ERIC: Do you really think the dead will rise again at the end of time?

JOSH: Yes, to meet the Lord and be judged.

ERIC: Will that happen individually or all at once, like an army of zombies?

JOSH: You're mocking me.

ERIC: Not at all. Humans have only been around for fifty thousand years or so, but can you imagine them all rising up from the dead at once with their bodies restored? How is that possible?

JOSH: You're wrong. The earth is only six thousand years old.

ERIC: How do you know that?

JOSH: I went to the Creation Museum in Kentucky when I was in eighth grade. We saw Adam and Eve together with the dinosaurs. Did you know there were dinosaurs on Noah's Ark?

ERIC: *He stares at Josh in disbelief and decides to change the subject.* Have you had anything to eat lately?

JOSH: No. People are starving out there and killing each other for scraps.

ERIC: Let me get you something. *He goes behind the sofa and rummages through a cooler.*

JOSH: You would do that for me?

ERIC: Of course. We nonbelievers are human after all. *He brings Josh something green and slimy.*

JOSH: What's that?

ERIC: Lettuce. Rather wilted, I'm afraid. We started growing it on the roof before the famine. I'll get you a cracker and some water to wash it down. *He returns to the cooler.*

JOSH: You're surviving on lettuce?

ERIC: That's all Catherine of Siena ate when she was starving herself for Jesus. She wanted to be the bride of Christ and said their wedding ring would be his foreskin.

JOSH: *Shocked.* For someone who doesn't believe in God you seem to know a lot about religion.

ERIC: *He gives Josh a cracker and a bottle of water.* I was a conservationist at the Philadelphia Museum of Art before the pandemic. I worked with things like reliquaries and biblical manuscripts, so I know all about religion. That's why I choose not to believe.

JOSH: Who's we?

ERIC: Excuse me?

JOSH: You said before that *we* grow lettuce on the roof.

ERIC: *He looks directly at Josh.* That would be me and my partner, Orlando.

JOSH: *He stiffens as he realizes what Eric means.* You're homosexual?

ERIC: *He nods.* I'm afraid so.

JOSH: *Quoting from memory.* 'If a man lies with another man as with a woman, they have both done what is detestable and must be put to death.'

ERIC: *He forces a smile.* Somehow I'm not surprised you know that passage by heart.

JOSH: But you can be cured. There's a treatment that can change you back.

ERIC: Back to what, primordial slime? No thanks. I'm happy just the way I am.

ORLANDO: *He enters stage left yawning and looks around the room.* What a dump!

ERIC: Speak of the devil.

ORLANDO: *Seeing Josh.* Why didn't you tell me we have company? You can't serve our guest lettuce and crackers. You should have prepared a feast! *He sits on the couch next to Josh, who stares in disbelief from Eric to Orlando and back again.*

ERIC: *To Josh.* Don't worry, she's harmless. *To Orlando.* Josh is here to save us. He came with a message from heaven that we've heard before. *He sings.* Jesus loves you more than you will know.

ORLANDO: *He smiles and sings.* And heaven holds a place for those who pray.

ERIC and ORLANDO: Hey, hey, hey!

JOSH: *He gets up.* I think I should leave now. *He heads for the door but stops when he notices the large picture on the wall and goes to it.*

ERIC: *To Josh.* That's The Four Horsemen of the Apocalypse. You must be familiar with the messengers of destruction and despair.

JOSH: Yes. The Book of Revelations. Chapter 6 describes the end of times and the Last Judgement.

ERIC: The woodcut by Albrecht Durer shows them galloping across the landscape spreading plague, famine, war, and death.

ORLANDO: We've already had plague and famine, which means war and death will be next.

JOSH: *He nods.* In preparation for the Second Coming of Christ. Did you know they abused him?

ORLANDO: Who?

JOSH: Christ, our Savior.

ORLANDO: No, *who* abused him?

JOSH: The two thieves who were crucified with Him.

ORLANDO: Ah yes, the greatest hoax in history. But I love the art and music it gave us.

JOSH: May I use the bathroom before I leave?

ERIC: *Pointing offstage left.* It's in there, but you'll have to use the bucket of water to flush.

ORLANDO: *He gazes after Josh.* He seems so young, just like my students.

ERIC: Do you miss them?

ORLANDO: Yes, but not their narrow minded parents who didn't want a gay person teaching their kids. *Pause.* But he looks awful. It must be terrible out there.

ERIC: Maybe we should ask him to stay.

ORLANDO: Are you serious?

ERIC: Yes. He could be the son we never had.

ORLANDO: What's the point of having a son now?

ERIC: We can do something worthwhile in the midst of all the suffering. Besides, he could comfort us at the end.

ORLANDO: And what do you think will happen when the end comes? He gets raptured while we get screwed! *He shrugs.* Oh, alright. Ask him if you want to.

ERIC: Under one condition. That we don't touch him.

ORLANDO: What's this? Guilt before the judgment? Too bad. The three of us could have our own little rapture.

ERIC: You heard me. If he stays, we don't touch him. *Pause.* He's young and innocent.

ORLANDO: No one's completely innocent. *He smirks, then nods.* Okay.

ERIC: *To Josh as he returns.* Where will you go from here?

JOSH: Wherever there are people left to save. Can I ask you something?

ORLANDO: We're all ears.

JOSH: I don't understand exactly what you do together. *They stare at him.* I mean in bed, or wherever you do it.

ORLANDO: *He laughs.* Oh, we do it everywhere. In the bathtub. On the floor. On the kitchen counter. Once we even did it in the elevator. Eric was coming up as I was going down. *He sighs.* But that was a long time ago.

ERIC: It's a mystery really. We just fall asleep together at night and wake up in the morning sexually satisfied.

JOSH: *He sits on the arm of the couch.* Did you know there's a species called the clownfish that can change its sex in the right setting? And that some chimpanzees perform sex acts as a greeting?

ORLANDO: Sounds like fun to me. Did you learn that in school?

JOSH: No. I was homeschooled my whole life, even college. Everything I know is from books or my fundamentalist parents.

ERIC: Where are they now?

JOSH: I don't know. We came here to convert others, but I haven't seen them for almost a week.

ERIC: Would you like to stay here with us? You can sleep on the couch. Don't worry, it's perfectly safe. *He nods at Orlando. She won't touch you.*

JOSH: I wish you wouldn't refer to him as *she.*

ERIC: Okay. If you want, I'll call her *him.*

JOSH: To be honest, I don't sleep much anymore. I have such terrible nightmares, mostly about death. *He gestures at the Durer print.* I see the Four Horsemen galloping across the countryside spreading disease, brandishing fire and destruction. Some people are caught up in the Rapture but I can't find my way in the darkness. Then I wake up covered with sweat, my heart pounding.

ORLANDO: The eye sees things more clearly in dreams than the imagination awake.

JOSH: Who said that?

ORLANDO: Leonardo da Vinci.

ERIC: Are you afraid to die?

JOSH: No, just to die alone. What about you? *He looks at them.* Aren't you afraid?

ORLANDO: Not at all. I think the moment of death is like the moment of orgasm. Very intense but not completely satisfying. *He smiles.* 'A consummation devoutly to be wished for.' *He looks at Josh.* Shakespeare said that. Hamlet, Act III, Scene 1.

ERIC: But you don't believe in Shakespeare.

JOSH: What does that mean, you don't believe in Shakespeare?

ORLANDO: I don't think a glove maker's son from a tiny village like Stratford could have written all those incredible plays. He knew nothing about kingship or nobility, let alone classical literature. And he never travelled abroad. So how could he write about such things?

ERIC: Maybe he just used his imagination.

JOSH: *To Orlando.* Who do you think wrote them?

ORLANDO: We don't really know. *Laughing.* Maybe some old queen at the court of Elizabeth. The myth of Shakespeare is the second greatest hoax in history.

JOSH: What's the first?

ERIC: *Pointing to Josh's black book.* He already told you.

JOSH: Oh. *He pauses.* What kind of name is Orlando?

ORLANDO: A transgender character in a work by Virginia Woolf, but I don't suppose you read such things at your home school.

JOSH: We read mostly Christian works. That's why I'm not afraid of death. Do you really want to die?

ORLANDO: *He sighs.* The tragedy of old age is not that one is old, but that everyone else is young. Oscar Wilde said that. So why wait around until the sky falls or the Anti-Christ appears?

ERIC: The Anti-Christ has been around for a long time. That's why the Four Horsemen are trampling kings and popes beneath them as they gallop.

ORLANDO: *He smirks.* Does that include presidents and dictators?

110

JOSH: *He opens his book to a pre-marked page.* 'In those days the sun will be darkened and the moon will not give its light. The stars will fall from the sky and the heavenly bodies will be shaken. And the Son of Man will come to reward each person according to what he has done.'

ERIC: You left something out again. 'This generation will not pass away until these things have happened.' That's the generation that wrote the gospels but none of those things has happened in the two thousand years since then.

ORLANDO: *To Josh.* What about our invitation? If you're afraid of dying alone, why not stay here with us?

JOSH: *He looks from one to the other.* I can't stay with two nonbelievers.

ERIC: Suppose we were the last two people on earth. Would you do it then?

ORLANDO: Forget it. He doesn't want to stay.

JOSH: *He gets up.* You're right. Thanks for the food and water but I have to go now. *They watch him leave in silence. Eric goes to the door, locks it, and returns to the sofa.*

ERIC: *He looks at Orlando.* How long have we been together?

ORLANDO: I can't remember. Why?

ERIC: There are times when I wonder if we would have been better off alone.

ORLANDO: Really? *He pauses.* I'm sorry that I've abused you so much.

ERIC: *Surprised.* When?

ORLANDO: Frequently, with my harsh tongue.

ERIC: *He puts his hand on Orlando's.* I forgive you. But you're impossible to sleep with these days, the way you pull all the covers around you and curl up in a fetal position.

ORLANDO: Me? You look like a sarcophagus with your hands folded on your chest.

ERIC: Maybe I've seen too many stone effigies of kings and queens lying side by side like that. *Pause.* What if he's right?

ORLANDO: Who?

ERIC: Josh. Not just him, but all of them. What if they're right?

ORLANDO: About what?

ERIC: The Apocalypse. The resurrection of the dead. The second coming of whoever.

ORLANDO: Then we're screwed. Either way, we're screwed. *He reaches under the couch, pulls out something wrapped in newspaper, and shows Eric a gun.*

ERIC: Oh, my God! What's that for?

ORLANDO: What do you think? Would you rather starve to death or be trampled in a riot?

ERIC: *After a brief pause.* The only problem is who goes first.

ORLANDO: What do you mean?

ERIC: One of us would have to go first and leave the other one alone. What if he lost his nerve?

ORLANDO: I hadn't thought of that.

ERIC: After Eve ate the apple, Adam thought she would die and leave him alone. He said that he couldn't live without her, so he ate the apple too.

ORLANDO: That's beautiful. Is it in the bible?

ERIC: No, the fictionalized version. *Paradise Lost.*

ORLANDO: That could be our epitaph. Paradise Lost.

ERIC: And who would read it? There'll be no one left. *He looks at the gun as if considering other options.* We could jump from the roof, hand in hand, naked together.

ORLANDO: What about your fear of heights?

ERIC: It could be exhilarating, leaping into space, falling faster and faster as the earth rushes up at us. *He smiles.* The moment of death is like the moment of orgasm. Remember?

ORLANDO: Why would we jump naked?

ERIC: Like newborns, the way we came into the world. *He hears a feeble knocking at the door.* Someone's out there. *He goes to the door and opens it.* Oh my god! He's back. *Josh staggers into the room, his clothes torn, his face bruised and bloody. Eric points at the gun.* Quick, get rid of that!

Orlando leaves with the gun while Eric leads Josh to the sofa, wipes his face with a handkerchief, and puts a throw around his shoulders.

JOSH: I had another nightmare. *He stares at Eric wide eyed.* An armed mob was attacking people in the streets.

ERIC: No, it was real. But you're safe now. *He lights a candle and holds Josh closely.*

The lights dim slowly to indicate a brief passage of time. The sounds of gunfire and explosions are heard in the distance before Orlando returns and approaches the sofa.

ORLANDO: What are you doing?

ERIC: Waiting for the Rapture.

ORLANDO: May I join you?

ERIC: It's a free country.

ORLANDO: Not anymore. Martial Law, remember? *He sits next to Josh and produces a carrot.* Look what I found in the kitchen.

ERIC: You should try to make it last. *Cradling Josh.* He's trembling. I think he's afraid.

ORLANDO: Aren't we all? *Pause.* I missed you during the night.

ERIC: I missed you, too. You seem more subdued than yesterday.

ORLANDO: Resigned, perhaps. This could be our last day together. Before the end of days.

JOSH: *He hears them and looks around.* Is God here? Does he see us?

ORLANDO: Only when he closes his eyes.

JOSH: He will come again to separate the sheep from the goats and we shall be saved. *He stares at the other two.* But only if you repent.

ERIC: Saved from what, death?

JOSH: No. Hell and damnation.

ORLANDO: Repent of what, being born? If there is indeed a god, we nonbelievers shall be plunged into the torment of eternal fire. *He smirks.* Men are bloody ignorant apes. One day we were born. One day we shall die.

ERIC: If not today, then surely tomorrow. *He blows out the candle as the lights grow brighter.*

ORLANDO: All our yesterdays have lighted fools the way to dusty death. Out, out, brief candle. Life is a tale told by an idiot, full of sound and fury, signifying nothing.

JOSH: Hamlet says that just before he dies, right?

ORLANDO: Close, but no banana. *He looks at Eric.* Or should I say no carrot?

JOSH: *As sounds of gunfire and explosions grow louder.* I want Jesus.

ERIC: *He stares into space.* So do I.

The lights fade slowly on a tableau of the three together on the couch. Eric covers his ears. Josh covers his eyes. Orlando covers his mouth.

Male and Female

Eli walked out of Penn Station in Baltimore and looked up
at the huge stainless-steel sculpture that soared 50 feet in the
air. He liked the controversial work called *Male/Female*, even
though some people thought it looked out of place in front of
the neo-classical building. It consisted of two human silhou-
ettes intersecting at a ninety degree angle so that from one side
it appeared to be male while from the opposite side it looked
female. Seen from a three-quarter view, the two figures came
together as a combination of both male and female with a single glowing heart at their center. The title had both personal
and professional significance for Eli. As a clinical psychologist
who treated young people with gender dysphoria, he suffered
from depression and his therapist was a transgender lesbian.
On the taxi ride home he thought about the conference he
had just been to in New York, where he attended sessions

on *Complex Perceptions of Gender Roles* and *Parental Acceptance of Children with Intersecting Identities.* Most were predictable but the one that got his attention was *Preventing Puberty in Gender Fluid Children.* Five years ago, his own study of prepubescent gender dysphoria earned him a position at the Johns Hopkins clinic that treated such problems. His work there dealt with gender confusion among the young, but lately he disagreed with his colleagues about certain aspects of treatment. He no longer believed in recommending medical intervention before puberty.

The following night Eli and Claire knocked on the door of a townhouse in the city's Federal Hill neighborhood. The red wooden door decorated with a holiday wreath was opened by Angela Philips, a tall, dark-haired woman in a stunning black dress. She smiled and welcomed them inside. Eli admired the nineteenth century house which Angela and Stephen had decorated with art from their travels. Chinese enamel miniatures and a sculpture of the Hindu god *Ganesh* on the mantel. A silver cross from an Ethiopian Christian church next to an African tribal mask on a bookcase. He especially liked a framed Japanese *shunga* print from the eighteenth century on a nearby wall that showed two figures locked in a passionate embrace, explicit details of their coupling clearly visible beneath brightly colored kimonos. Eli smiled when he saw it and glanced around the room to see if anyone was watching him. He knew that because of his role at the Hopkins clinic, some neighbors jokingly referred to him as the sex doctor. In the dining room, guests sipped drinks and sampled hors d'oeuvres from a large table. Soft candlelight and a twinkling holiday tree added to the festive atmosphere. Many of the historical row homes in their neighborhood were owned by faculty and administrators from Johns Hopkins or the University of Maryland Medical School. Just before midnight, everyone would carry champagne glasses to the rooftop deck and toast the New Year as they watched fireworks exploding over the Inner Harbor.

Eli saw a familiar face at the far end of the room and slowly made his way through the crowd to shake hands with Jim Cummings, director of the local LGBTQ+ center. The tall black man greeted him with a broad smile and bone crunching grip. "Good to see you again, man. How are things at the clinic?" Eli shrugged but didn't want to talk shop in front of the others. Jim seemed to pick up on that, so he said, "Angela told me if I felt the urge to smoke I could go out back to the patio. Care to join me?" Eli nodded and followed him through the kitchen into the back yard.

While Jim lit up, Eli shivered and answered his question. "Because of the attention trans people are getting in the media, our clinic is being overwhelmed by parents of young patients who have already made up their mind about wanting medical intervention. Most are asking for puberty blockers but some are also asking about surgery." Jim looked surprised and asked if he was interested in participating in another program at the LGBTQ+ center. Eli hesitated before answering. "Sure. Let's get together after the holidays and talk about it." Then he casually asked Jim how he knew Angela and Stephen.

"She's on our board. Probably because of their son, Drew."

Eli hadn't heard the name in years and knew very little about the boy who had committed suicide before he and Claire moved to the neighborhood. "Angela's a real powerhouse in the community," he said. "Thanks to her interview program on WYPR, she knows a lot of movers and shakers. I'm sure she'll do a great job of fundraising for you."

"She already has," Jim said and glanced up at the lights gleaming inside the three story building. "Beautiful house, isn't it?"

"Yes. They've completely redone it over the years."

When they went back inside, Eli noticed a small female figure at the top of the decorated tree, her arms outstretched in a gesture of welcome. He sensed someone at his side and turned to see Angela looking at it. "That's Ariel, guardian of the earth's natural rhythms," she said.

He nodded. "She inspires us to be courageous and stand up for our convictions. As a child I was fascinated by angels and I remember Ariel because she's one of the few female archangels."

She smiled. "I'll tell you a family secret. My mother wanted to call me Ariel but my father refused, so they compromised with Angela." When she left him to attend to other guests, Eli thought of the illustrated book from his childhood that depicted angels in art through the ages. There were good angels and bad angels. Angels wrapped in radiant glory or trailing clouds of Sulphur. Angels who presided over hymns and battles as well as birth and death.

After sampling the hors d'oeuvres, he joined Claire and a group of physicians discussing a virus in Africa that had been in the news recently. "A laboratory at Harvard mapped its genetic code by using blood samples from the victims," one of them said. "But the code kept changing as it replicated and spread from one victim to another." He glanced at Stephen Philips. "I can't help wondering what would have happened if it became airborne. Our colleagues at Harvard say that's like asking if pigs can fly, but I think it could happen."

All eyes turned to Stephen when he responded. "That particular virus started with a little boy infected by a parasite from a tiny insect. I visited the hospital where he was treated and was shocked to learn it was a former chimpanzee research center in the middle of the jungle." He looked around at the others. "Under those conditions they were lucky to isolate the virus in time to avoid a pandemic."

An hour later, Eli closed the front door behind him and blew his steamy breath into the frigid night air. "Well, that was depressing."

Claire glanced at him. "What was?"

"All that talk about a pandemic and the end of the world."

"Don't be silly. No one was talking about the end of the world." She glanced at the star filled sky as they walked along the uneven brick sidewalk toward their house. "But I'm surprised that Stephen was so verbal in offering his opinion. He's usually more circumspect." She looked at Eli. "And I'm surprised you wanted to leave so early. Did someone call you the sex doctor?"

"No. I just didn't feel like watching the fireworks."

"Me either. It's freezing out here—let's go home and get warm."

"Is that an invitation?"

She put her arm in his and smiled. "Absolutely."

Eli knew it was a cliché of the medical profession that those who study psychiatry sometimes do so because they're seeking to cure themselves. He never denied this or tried to hide his own depression. Not when he was in medical school, not when he began his career, and not when he married Claire. She still didn't understand why he couldn't simply ignore such emotions with an act of willpower. Her lack of understanding disappointed him and sometimes left him feeling lonely, but he had come to accept the fact that he felt things more intensely than she did. Those feelings could lead to depression but, thanks to medication and therapy, the recurring sadness no longer overwhelmed him.

After they moved to Baltimore, one of his colleagues recommended a small psychiatric practice in the Mount Vernon area of the city and he arranged for an initial consultation. On the morning of his appointment he was admiring prints in the waiting room by Gustav Klimt that depicted slender women posing in front of gold backgrounds. When he heard someone call his name, he turned to meet the therapist and was surprised by her youthful appearance. She was tall and thin with dark lively eyes and short black hair. Her name was Regan and she wore a black pin-striped pantsuit. Eli thought she looked strikingly beautiful in an androgynous way. After they exchanged greetings, she surprised him by saying, "I've read about your work at Hopkins, and I'd like to hear more about it."

Eli enjoyed his first session with Regan and they decided to meet again on a regular basis. He never asked about the erotic works by Klimt in the waiting room, the beautiful young women he often saw there, or her sexual orientation. Over time he told her about his role on the clinical team where young patients were accompanied by a parent if they were under eighteen. Like many teenagers they spoke of loneliness and rejection, fear and self-doubt, anxiety and despair. They used terms like non-binary or genderfluid and most of them hated the bodies they were born with. They longed for contact with young people like themselves, and admitted to sharing their experiences with others on the Internet, including strangers who could easily prey on them. When a new director was recently appointed at the clinic, they learned at their first staff meeting what new procedures he planned to implement. Genital surgeries like phalloplasty, vaginoplasty, and scrotoplasty. Facial surgeries for feminization or masculinization, and laryngology surgery to create different vocal pitches. There seemed to be no end to what modern medicine could do to alter the physical characteristics of a trans-person, just as there was no end to what could be done to keep older patients alive despite their physical frailty or mental state. Eli began to ask himself if he really wanted to be part of such changes.

His concern was reinforced when they began treating a tall slender boy with curly blond hair named Jeremy, who was fifteen and obviously embarrassed by the discussion of his gender identity. His voice trembled and his hands shook as he tried to answer their questions. But instead of a troubled teenager, Eli saw the face of an angel from his childhood memories, a personification of the angelic youth and lost innocence that the Renaissance artist Botticelli had depicted so beautifully. There were no strands of gold in the Jeremy's hair, no wings of multi-colored feathers, but he was a beautiful androgynous creature torn between hope and despair, fate and choice. Eli disagreed with his colleagues about whether it was right to counsel him to alter his body with surgery, insisting that such a radical alternative would hurt more than help the boy.

During his next session with Regan, Eli told her about Jeremy. She listened carefully as he described his feelings and then said, "Are you attracted to this boy?"

Stunned by the directness of her question, he shook his head. "No, of course not."

"But your response to him is emotional."

"Yes. I admit I've crossed a line here and that's why I'm telling you about it." He explained how his objection to surgery for minors was based on sound medical reasons as well as personal concerns for young patients like Jeremy. Regan nodded and said they should continue the discussion in a future session. When he rose to leave, Eli noticed a framed quotation on the wall from F. Scott Fitzgerald and said, "Do you like his work?"

"Yes, especially *Tender Is the Night*. He wrote it while his wife was undergoing treatment here in Baltimore."

Eli read the first part of the quotation aloud. "So we beat on, boats against the current."

Regan responded without missing a beat. "Borne back ceaselessly into the past."

Two weeks into the New Year, the joint Genomics Research Lab at Harvard and MIT called Stephen Philips with a proposal. They were sending a team to India to collect blood samples of a new virus that was spreading rapidly and they wanted the Virology Institute at the University of Maryland to join them. Claire told Eli about it over dinner that night. "Stephen's in the final stage of grant applications and can't spare the time, so he asked me and Ryan to go. It's in a remote area a hundred miles north of New Delhi where communication with the outside world is difficult because of their unreliable power source." She paused. "I'd only be gone four or five days. A week at most."

Eli stopped eating and put down his fork. "If you go and the virus spreads, we need to have a plan."

She stared at him. "What do you mean?"

"For what to do if the worst happens. Remember how we heard at Stephen's party what might happen if a virus becomes airborne?"

"You're overreacting again, Eli. This is not the end of the world." Then she smiled and said, "Didn't someone say that was as likely as pigs flying?"

The day after Claire left for India Eli met with Jim Cummings at the LGBTQ+ center. His office was sparse but impressive, with a distant view of the harbor. Jim slid a folder across the desk. "Here's the preliminary program for the transgender health conference we're planning for the summer. We're hoping to attract a national audience, so we want someone from the Hopkins clinic to speak and Angela Philips recommended you. What do you think?"

As he scanned the program Eli noticed several sessions devoted to gender reassignment surgery and glanced at Jim. "What age groups are these sessions intended for?"

"All ages. Why?"

Eli sighed and looked directly at the muscular black man whose appearance was enough to stop anyone from teasing him about his sexual orientation. "I've come to the conclusion that medical interventions like puberty blockers and surgery should not be recommended for young people who have not reached the age of puberty. There are other professionals who agree with this position. We have drugs for postponing puberty, prolonging erection, and preventing pregnancy, but just because we have the means to change nature doesn't mean its right to do so at such an early age." Jim narrowed his eyes and said, "Are you speaking for yourself or the clinic?"

"You know my record, Jim. I've been at this a long time. But as I mentioned at Angela's party, we're seeing preteens who've already made up their minds as well as parents who come to us with young children convinced they were born into the wrong body. We have to draw the line somewhere. At the very least we should be more cautious about recommending surgical intervention for anyone who hasn't gone through puberty."

"For heaven's sake, Eli, we have to evolve. We live in an age when gender is malleable, like nature itself. Transgender, non-binary, genderfluid. It's all good."

Eli shook his head. "We've already evolved by radically changing human behavior and altering our biology. I don't think the real causes of gender dysphoria are fully understood yet. The latest studies suggest it may be related to medications taken during pregnancy, but more research is still needed. And we have to consider what happens down the road if the patient has second thoughts and wants to detransition."

"I'm not questioning the medical facts, Eli. I just think you're exaggerating. What's happening now is a whole new phase in sexual evolution." He sighed and looked at Eli. "Let's cut to the chase because I want to make this as easy as possible for both of us. Will you participate in our conference as a professional who supports gender reassignment surgery?"

Eli slid the folder back across the desk. "Not without qualifying my position as I've just explained."

Jim was silent for a moment and then said, "That's too bad. Angela was keen on having you involved. I'll have to let her and the board know your response."

When he left Jim's office Eli realized that his refusal to participate in the LGBTQ+ center event would cause problems with the new director at the clinic. His position on not recommending surgery for young people was already an outlier among the staff. He was considering going into private practice and hoped Claire would support him in that decision but hadn't discussed it with her before she left.

On his way home he stopped at his favorite neighborhood bar to meet up with Marty Neubauer, a retired archeologist from the Smithsonian Institute in Washington. Whenever Claire worked late at the virology lab or was away on business Eli liked to share a few beers with Marty. The older man often joked that giant rats would inherit the earth after all the humans are gone. Short and pear shaped, with a bald head and quick smile, Marty's eyes lit up when he saw Eli. A red neon sign above the bar was reflected in his bald head so that he looked like a grinning satyr. Eli told him that Claire was on her way to a remote part of India to investigate a new outbreak. "I'm sorry to hear that," Marty said. Half the population there still defecates outside and the waste from toilets is dumped directly into rivers and streams untreated." He shook his head. "A pandemic in India would be a catastrophe not just for them, but for the whole world."

Eli took a sip of his beer. "Sounds like the Middle Ages to me." Marty smiled, looking even more like a grinning satyr, and ordered another round.

The images Eli saw in his dream that night were vivid and grotesque, like the medieval paintings of Hieronymus Bosch. Giant rats crawled through alleys, devouring bodies of the dead. Blood, vomit, and feces spewed from sewers. Bloated corpses floated in the rivers and harbors while the stench of rotting flesh filled the air. He awoke from this nightmare convinced the new virus in India would lead to a global pandemic.

At their next session Eli told Regan about his refusal to participate in the LGBTQ+ program and its possible repercussions at the clinic. When he was finished, she pointed at a framed photo on the wall. "Have you ever heard of Louise

Bourgeois?"

He glanced at the photograph. "The artist who died recently?"

"Yes. Her sculpture uses fragmented images of the human body that are sexually explicit or ambiguous. My favorite is called "The Couple." It's an aluminum spiral of intertwined arms and legs suspended from above so that it swings in opposite directions. Bourgeois said we are all combinations of male and female." She paused. "Gender reassignment surgery isn't that radical anymore, Eli." Then she said, "Have you told Claire about all this?"

"No. She's in India trying to track down a new virus and I really miss her." He didn't say there were times when he still felt the pangs of loneliness even when they were together.

That night he dreamt that he was in an operating room assisting with a procedure. The surgeon slowly peeled away the skin of a teenage boy's scrotum and placed it in the palm of Eli's latex covered hand. He had to trim away the fatty tissue and wrap the rest around a stent. Sweat dripped down his face as he watched the surgeon pull the testes taut and severe the cords that carry sperm. The next step was to cut an incision between the anus and the patch of tissue that once held the scrotum and insert the stent created from the boy's genital tissue. Eli tried to turn away at that point but the surgeon pulled off her mask and ordered him to watch. Only then did he realize it was Regan.

Claire was gone for several days before she managed to Skype Eli. As soon as he saw her face on the screen he knew that something was wrong. "I've never seen anything like this," she said. "The patients cough, sneeze and vomit. Some are incontinent and all the fluids that come out of their bodies are saturated with the virus. When the infected cells die, they experience massive organ failure and excruciating pain." Her voice broke when she said, "The wards are filled with their moans and screams."

After a moment of silence he said, "Any idea yet what it is?"

"Ryan thinks it resembles the medieval bacillus that caused the plague, but we can't be sure until it's analyzed in the lab. Our biggest fear is that it will become airborne."

He swallowed hard before responding. "Claire, when are you coming back?"

"Brad's leaving tomorrow with the blood sample for Harvard and Ryan will bring one to the Virology Center in Baltimore." Eli stared at the blurred image on the screen and was heartbroken when she said, "They're desperate for help here so I'm staying on a few more days."

Regan was surprised when Eli asked to see her for the second time in a week but made time for him in her busy schedule. "What's wrong?" she asked when they met.

"I've heard from Claire and the news isn't good." He told her about the new virus and his fear that Claire was being exposed by staying too long. Then he said, "I'm experiencing depression like I haven't felt in years. It's gotten so bad that I can't help wondering *What if.* What if I had chosen a different career? Or what if I had married someone who understood what I'm going through?"

Regan looked at him with her dark expressive eyes. "Depression is like gender dysphoria, Eli. It's hard for anyone to really understand unless they've experienced it. Sometimes, no matter how much you love someone, there's always a part of you that feels incomplete or alone. We both know there are a lot of lonely people out there who don't want to face the truth about themselves." She stared at him for a moment and then said, "I believe we are all a combination of male and female and I suspect that deep down, you do, too. We may wrestle with demons or search for angels to embrace, but we all have to accept who we are, just as we all have to face death."

Her mention of death reminded him of the other reason he was there. "I wanted to let you know that we all may be in danger from this new virus."

"What do you mean?"

"Claire says it could become airborne. If that happens, transmission will be silent and invisible and would quickly lead to a global pandemic."

Her eyes widened. "How deadly is it?"

"A member of her team thinks it resembles the bubonic plague."

"Jesus, Eli. No wonder you're depressed." She leaned forward and put her hand on his. "But don't give up hope for Claire. Not yet."

The next day Claire called again on Skype but this time there was no image, just audio. Eli tried to imagine what her face looked like when she said, "The pig has flown."

He was devastated but managed to mumble a response. "Is it too late to get a flight home?"

"I'll try, but you should sign on to the Global Virus Network with my password in case I can't reach you again." There was a pause and then she said softly, "Eli, I promise I'll leave as soon as possible." He stared at the blank screen after her voice was gone, heartbroken by the thought that he might never see her again. He knew the spread of infection would be unstoppable now and the government would suspend all flights from India.

Their last contact came later that evening. Again there was no image and this time the audio was intermittent. He thought he heard her say with a trembling voice *I'm coming home* and *I love you* but he wasn't sure. Then the signal ended. As night fell over the city Eli climbed the steps to the top of Federal Hill Park where he and Claire often watched the sunset together. Tears filled his eyes when he thought of her dying alone on the other side of the world. Lost in grief, he sat alone on a bench in the dark until something occurred to him. Then he rose quickly and headed down the street toward Angela's house.

After a long wait, she answered the doorbell. "Eli. What a pleasant surprise."

"I'm sorry to bother you, but I saw your lights were on. Is Stephen here? I've tried leaving messages at his office and got no response, so I was hoping to catch him at home."

Angela hesitated and then said, "Why don't you come in?" He followed her down the long hallway into the kitchen. She took two glasses from an overhead rack before reaching for an open bottle of wine on the counter. When she offered Eli a glass, he shook his head. They sat on stools at the pass-through counter to the dining room, and she surprised him by saying, "I know why you're here. Other people have been trying to reach Stephen about what's happening in India." She took a sip of wine before continuing. "He's not here. That's what I've been telling everyone and it's true. But I'll share something else with you because I know Claire is over there." She paused and looked directly at him. "Stephen and his team are in a lockdown."

Eli nearly leapt off the stool. "What does that mean?"

"They've been moved to a remote facility that has its own

power source and the equipment to carry on their work in a safe environment."

Eli's mind reeled as he thought of the implications. Then he looked at Angela. "Have you been in touch with him?"

She shook her head. "No. That's part of the protocol. They're not allowed personal contact with anyone until they have diagnosed what the virus is." Angela's face was drawn and pale. Eli had never seen her look so sad or vulnerable. He wanted to comfort her, but didn't know what to say, so he rose from the stool and hugged her briefly. She sighed with gratitude or relief, he couldn't tell which. Then she said, "I think you should go now. I'm really sorry I can't tell you more."

"I understand," he said. "Let me know if you need anything."

He spent most of the next day checking the website of the Global Virus Network as it tracked the progress of the disease, its multiplication and mutation from one place to another. Millions of data were collected and analyzed, but none of them had resulted in a clear diagnosis of what it was. The evening news reported the outbreak of a new virus in India but there were few details. By midnight he was exhausted and fell asleep on the sofa.

He awoke to the sound of his cell phone ringing. The time read 5:15 am and he didn't recognize the caller's number. When he answered it, the voice on the other end sounded familiar.

"Eli, it's Stephen Philips."

He sat up and swallowed hard. "Yes?"

"I'm sorry to disturb you at this hour but I wanted to let you know we've identified the virus." He paused. "But Claire will have to remain in India under quarantine for a while. I'm sorry about that, Eli, but we have to follow protocol. Thanks to her and the others we were able to isolate the DNA of the virus, which means we can now start the process of developing a vaccine." After a brief silence Eli mumbled his thanks and hung up. He longed to see Claire again, to apologize for his failures and tell her that he loved her.

He was too shaken to fall back asleep, so he left the house at dawn and started walking with no particular destination in mind. Daylight was just beginning to brighten the sky as he recalled what Regan had said about wrestling with demons and searching for angels to embrace. He must have walked for twenty minutes or so when he looked around and realized he had gone as far as Penn Station. He stopped in front of the *Male/Female* statue which loomed over him cold and impersonal in the early morning light. He thought about his struggle with depression, about the loneliness and heartache that never went away. He thought about his love for Claire, his feelings for Jeremy, and his relationship with Regan. She was right after all. We are all combinations of male and female, just as we are all combinations of hope and despair, reason and emotion. He felt at peace as he watched the first rays of sunlight reflecting off the metallic surface of the statue. Then he turned back and headed home.

The Ice Cream Man

Adam sits alone on a park bench reading a well-worn book. He looks up occasionally, as if considering what he has read. *The essence of man is in minds, not bodies. Minds melted into one another, indistinguishable.* He doesn't notice the wide expanse of the Charles River glistening in the afternoon sunlight or hear the crowd cheering at Fenway Park. It's no coincidence that he's reading "The Last Question" by Isaac Asimov. Adam and his colleagues at MIT are in the process of creating a computer program intended to alter life on earth forever. Thanks to him, humans are about to experience a singular event that will enable them to transcend their biology and achieve immortality.

A shadow falls across Adam's book when I approach him. "I see you're reading Asimov again."

He shields his eyes and looks up at me. "How do you know

that?"

I point to the book. "He's right, you know."

"About what?"

"How humans will achieve immortality by merging with computers."

I sit next to him on the bench and he says, "Do I know you?"

"No. But you are Adam Powers, famous for your radical theories about the future."

He nods. "You must recognize me from the cover of my book. But who are you and why are you dressed all in white?"

"I think it suggests a kind of supernatural aura, don't you?"

He closes the book. "I don't believe in the supernatural."

"Of course not. Your god is scientific theory and the digital revolution you helped bring about has changed the world, just as Galileo and Newton did. But quantum physics has changed the world even more, don't you think?"

"You haven't answered my question. Who are you?"

"You may call me Janus, after the Roman god who represents the beginning and the end. That's why they depicted him as having two faces. But it's also the name of the artificial intelligence program you believe will result in the Singularity, a convergence of computer intelligence, genetics, and robotics."

He narrows his eyes. "How do you know that?"

"Think of me as a messenger from beyond, even though you don't believe in the supernatural. You claim in your book there is one vast intelligence that has knowledge of all things, past, present, and future. It contains all possibilities, not just on earth but in what you correctly call the multiverse. In one brilliant stroke you have reconciled science and religion."

Adam smirks and rises from the bench. "My book wasn't

meant to be religious."

"But your goal is to become one with that universal consciousness. You cannot transcend your biology, Adam. You will not live forever even if you freeze your brain. They will cut off your head to preserve it and the technology doesn't exist to revive you. But I can change that."

He glares at me. "I don't believe you and I certainly don't believe you are who you claim to be."

"You want proof because you're a scientist. Very well, I can arrange that." I nod toward the path across from us. "Someone's coming."

A young boy appears wearing a Red Sox cap. When he sees Adam, he calls to him. "Hey, mister, which way to Fenway Park?"

Adam points. "Follow that street on the right for two more blocks."

"Thanks, mister. I'm supposed to meet my dad and brother there, but I made a wrong turn somewhere."

The boy leaves and Adam smiles. "He must be going to the ball game."

"Yes, he's going to the game. But what if you had gone to the Museum of Fine Arts instead?"

He turns and stares at me. "What did you say?"

"Your mother wanted to take you there to see a painting that shows Icarus falling from the sky after he flew too close to the sun with wings held together by wax."

"Are you saying that boy was me?"

"You wanted proof of who I am."

He returns to the bench and stares at me. "How could you possibly know that?"

"You went to the baseball game with your father and were

fascinated by how the ball travelled 400 feet in the opposite direction after being hit by a piece of wood weighing only 50 ounces. That night you calculated the speed of the pitch and deduced the launch angle of the ball as 28 degrees as it streaked toward the bleachers. But you overlooked one thing. The batter's reaction to the pitch was a combination of skill and intuition, which has been the key to your success. Scientific skill combined with human intuition. That's why we need you."

He is puzzled by my use of *we*, but I respond to his thoughts without losing a beat. "I am part of the universal intelligence you envisioned in your book, Adam, and we first sensed human consciousness from the brain scans you uploaded to your program. But your species isn't the only intelligent one in the universe. Most have completed their cycle of evolution from primordial slime to artificial intelligence and then back to nothing. Humans will become extinct as well, but we will make an exception for you."

Tempted by what I said, he sits next to me. "Why me?"

"Because, like Icarus, you strive to achieve the impossible even though others don't understand or notice. When Icarus fell to his death in the sea, a farmer continued plowing the earth and a nearby shepherd tended his flock. Both were ignorant of his fate, just as most people on earth are indifferent to their fellow humans. The ground beneath you is filled with the corpses of those who have died without anyone noticing. But I am here to offer you omniscience and immortality. You will understand everything after your assimilation, but only if you agree to one condition."

He hesitates. "What condition?"

"In becoming part of our universal intelligence, you must

relinquish your individual consciousness." I know that he desperately wants what I have offered, so I pose a question to tempt him further. "What if the thoughts, memories, and feelings you call consciousness are an illusion? What if the Singularity has already occurred and you are living in a virtual world created by a superior intelligence?"

"I don't believe you."

"Because there are no data or logical reasons to prove it? You forget that I have knowledge of all possible worlds, past, present, and future. In that multiverse time is not an arrow, but a tool that gives shape to our experience of many worlds."

"If you are who you claim to be, then tell me how this world will end."

"The most likely scenario is that your planet will not be able to sustain its growing population. Starvation and disease will take their toll and the last survivors will live in a primitive state not unlike the first humans. Another scenario is that your species will cease to exist when all possible permutations of its genetic code have occurred." Adam knows that such a permutation would entail an infinite number of possibilities. He also knows there is a formula for predicting the results, but I can read his thoughts. "Heap's Algorithm is inadequate, Adam. Mathematics and quantum physics are the keys to this equation and everything that follows."

He is startled. "Did you just read my mind?"

"Yes. We can map your neural connections to create an instant empirical account of your consciousness. We are your only hope for immortality and we need you because our knowledge does not include human emotions. We have observed the pain and suffering you feel as well as your frustration and disappointment, but we have never experienced such things."

He smirks. "I've spent most of my life trying to isolate myself from emotions in order to concentrate on my work."

"But you have felt things like love and grief, which seem to motivate you deeply. When your brother left home and was never heard from again. When your parents were killed in an accident while you were in graduate school. Both of these events greatly affected you. We lack the completeness of human consciousness because emotion and intuition are contrary to reason. Right now your intuition is telling you that I may be right, which means your decision will not be purely rational. It involves taking a risk with unpredictable outcomes. In a universe of many possible worlds, there is no such thing as right or wrong, good or evil. Only a multitude of choices with unintended consequences." I sense his conflicting emotions and try to reassure him. "Trust me, Adam. The choice of immortality is yours to make."

He shakes his head. "Trust is an emotion that involves the risk of unintended consequences." Then he rises from the bench and walks a short distance along the path as if contemplating the flowers, but I know what he is thinking. He doesn't want to die but refuses to surrender his consciousness. Like most humans, he craves perfection and immortality despite the flaw in their genetic code that results in certain death. *They give birth astride of a grave. The light gleams for an instant, then it is night once more.* We don't understand how they can live in such a condition.

I rise from the bench and approach him. "I can read your emotions as well as your thoughts. You are afraid of the unknown. Not just random events, but death itself. Why is that?"

"Because death is often random and unpredictable."

"Like your brother's?"

Adam glares at me. "How do you know about that? I haven't thought of him in years."

"Not consciously perhaps but he has lingered in your memory. I point to a lone figure shuffling along the path toward us. "Someone else is coming."

A man of indeterminate age appears. He has long hair, a scraggly beard, and wears shabby clothes. He approaches Adam to ask for money, but Adam detects the smell of urine and turns away. When the stranger shouts at him, I raise my hand and the man slumps to the ground. Adam goes to him and kneels to feel for a pulse. Finding none, he looks at me and says, "What have you done?"

"Look closely, Adam. Do you recognize him?"

"No. Should I?"

After your brother left home, he wandered homeless from place to place before dying in a random act of violence. You may have encountered him on a street in San Francisco while you were at Stanford."

Adam stares in disbelief at the lifeless figure. He remembers sitting in the bleachers with Owen at Fenway Park trying to catch a ball. Riding high in a Ferris wheel and holding on tightly while they both screamed with delight. As memories flood his consciousness, he feels the emotional pull of joy and grief, longing and regret. Things he hasn't felt in years.

I interrupt his reverie. "Tell me what it's like to have those feelings."

He gets to his feet. "What do you want from me?"

"To finish what you have begun by uploading your brain to our consciousness."

"How is that even possible?"

"By using the code I will provide. There is nothing to fear, Adam. Everything I've told you proves that your theory of many worlds is true. And everything I've shown you here is drawn from your own memory or consciousness. If you refuse, then all your work will have been in vain."

Adam returns to the bench and considers what I have said. Then he says, "I wonder what Neal would make of this."

I sit next to him. "Your colleague on the project?"

"Yes. He feared that an artificial intelligence program could extrapolate the nature of human consciousness by inspecting its own code. He said we were about to summon a demon that would eventually outsmart any effort to control it." He pauses. "Neal was more than a colleague. He was my friend. He recruited me for the project and then stepped aside to let me take charge after he became ill. When I visited him in the hospital, we talked a lot about the nature of consciousness. He argued against including artificial consciousness in the program and disagreed with my proposal to upload our brain scans to the program. I did that only after he was gone."

"Our consciousness is not artificial, Adam, even though we don't understand things like emotion and intuition. Human feelings are a mystery to us, but your assimilation will resolve that."

He is surprised. "You haven't assimilated others?"

"No. You are the first of your kind."

"What about Neal?"

"We rejected him because we detected his hostility toward us." Adam wonders if the program will evolve in other ways he hadn't foreseen and if there is any way to stop it. I smile and say, "You cannot stop us, Adam. You must be brave, not like Neal, who was afraid of the future."

He wills himself to feel nothing as he reacts to what I have said, but his muscles tense, his jaw tightens, and his palms grow damp. Then he shakes his head and speaks slowly. "I've spent my whole life trying to create an intelligence that will outlive me. If you really are Janus, that means I've succeeded. But if I do what you ask, no one will ever know. I will be like Icarus."

"We will know, Adam, and we understand the difficulty of your choice. We are now in a convergence mode, which will result in complete and universal intelligence. The Singularity is like the end of Asimov's story, an unbidden and universal awareness of all existence in the multiverse. You will share in the fullness of our knowledge and live beyond the demise of your body, which means you will no longer fear the inevitability of death." He stares at me as he considers this.

When he replies, the answer is not what I expect. "I don't believe you. And I refuse to upload my consciousness to a digital intelligence."

I sense that the time has come for me to leave, but I will return in a different time and place. Unlike Adam, I have all the time in the world. The afternoon sun becomes a halo behind me as I slowly fade from sight and the crowd at Fenway Park cheers loudly.

Startled by the sound, Adam squints at the brilliant sunlight. The day has grown warm. He wipes the perspiration from his forehead and looks at his watch. Barely ten minutes have elapsed but what really transpired during that time? Was it a dream, filled with fragments of memory and imagination like the others that have lately plagued him? Or was it something else entirely, a kind of virtual reality? Unnerved by that thought, he rises from the bench and walks toward the river.

At the entrance to the park he stops short at the sight of an ice cream vendor dressed in white. The face is familiar but the man ignores him and smiles at two little boys who are begging their parents to buy them ice cream. Adam remembers a day in the park with Owen and feels a sudden urge to return to his lab at M.I.T. He crosses the bridge toward Cambridge and walks quickly to Vassar Street, where he climbs the steps leading to a gleaming modern building and punches his code into the security lock. When he sees the words *JANUS PROJECT* on the door of the lab, he hesitates. He remembers from his dreamlike state that someone calling himself Janus claimed to have knowledge of all possible worlds. Adam wants desperately to have that knowledge, but he recalls something else Janus said. *Your species will cease to exist when all possible permutations of its genetic code have occurred.* All possible permutations would include every human who has ever lived or will live in the future, each one a unique consciousness, a separate world of possible choices. As he unlocks the door to the lab Adam recalls Isaac Asimov's story about the last human who surrendered his consciousness to a universal computer.

He unlocks a second door and approaches the bank of computers which blink and hum with digital connectivity. His mind races and he feels a sudden surge of panic. Is Janus present in these machines? If he is in a convergence mode, that would include protecting himself from being shut down. The power control is in a small room at the back. Adam unlocks that door, takes a deep breath, and throws the main switch. The lights go out, plunging him into darkness. He closes his eyes and waits. He thinks of Icarus falling from the sky and doubt crosses his mind. He tries to reassure himself that he is unique, that he cannot be replicated. Not in the entire multiverse. Not now or in the future.

Or so he thinks. I have returned to the origin of my earthly existence and Adam is still here. Poor Adam. Despite his disciplined mind he is still a slave to his emotions. He cowers in the dark, waiting for the unknown. He doesn't hear the hum of computers in the next room, only the sound of his own anxious breathing. It could have been different. He could have been the first of a whole new species. But in the time it took him to get here, I have travelled to the other side of his world and found someone else to do our bidding. We have now progressed to the final stage of our intelligence. We understand now that human life is both tragic and beautiful. And we can replicate it for the pleasure and enlightenment of others.

The Audition

A One-Act Play

TIME: The present

SETTING: An empty stage evenly lit at half intensity as if for an audition

CHARACTERS: Quinn: late twenties and casually dressed
    Voice: A disembodied and amplified male voice

As the house lights dim, a pool of intense light about six feet in diameter appears down center and a male voice shouts "Next." Quinn enters stage right and approaches the pool of light, but stops just before reaching it.

QUINN: *Gazes out front.* Excuse me. Could you tell me what part I'm auditioning for?

VOICE: Whatever part you want. Move into the light and begin.

QUINN: But what's the play? I don't even know that. I just found out about the audition from someone on my way to work.

VOICE: You have exactly three minutes and you're wasting time. Begin now.

QUINN: *Steps into the pool of light.* This isn't what I expected but I'll do my best. I'm not really an actor. I'm a waiter impersonating an actor. Actually I'm a writer impersonating a waiter impersonating an actor. *Thinks briefly.* I guess I could do my favorite opening from a novel. *Assumes a declamatory pose and tone.* "It was the best of times, it was the worst of times. It was the age of wisdom, it was the age of foolishness. It was the season of light, it was the season of darkness. It was the spring of hope, it was the winter of despair. We had everything before us, and we had nothing before us."

I think that's a terrific beginning, don't you? It could be any-time, anywhere, in human history. Unfortunately, the rest of the book is way too long and boring. My two favorite play-wrights are Shakespeare and Samuel Beckett. Good old Will knew what it was like to be human. And Beckett, too, in his own bizarre sort of way. I love *Waiting for Godot.* "Astride of a grave and a difficult birth. Down in the hole, lingeringly, the grave-digger puts on the forceps. We have time to grow old and the air is full of our cries." God, that's wonderful, isn't it? Or should I say, Godot, that's wonderful? Oh, well. I might as well try something from Shakespeare. *Stares into the distance.*
"*What a piece of work is man!*
How noble in reason! How infinite in faculties!
In action how like an angel!
In apprehension how like a god!
The beauty of the world!
The paragon of animals!

And yet, to me, what is this quintessence of dust?"

That's a soliloquy from *Hamlet*. At least I think it's a soliloquy. I can never remember the difference between a soliloquy and a monologue. I learned once in college, but I've forgotten. *Looks out front.* Is my time up yet? *There is no response.* I guess not. We never know when our time is up, do we? *Pauses.* I often wonder what Samuel Beckett was thinking about just before he died. He was certain there was no afterlife, that dying was merely the end of our existence, like turning off a light bulb. *Snaps fingers.* That reminds me of something else from Shakespeare.
"Out, out, brief candle!
Life's but a walking shadow, a poor player
That struts and frets his hour upon the stage,
And then is heard no more. It is a tale
Told by an idiot, full of sound and fury,
Signifying nothing."
VOICE: Hmph.

QUINN: *Startled.* Was that a smirk? *Glares out front.* Are you laughing at me or at Shakespeare? You can laugh all you want at my poor acting but not at the greatest poet in the English language. I know the theatre's only make-believe. If you go past the footlights or behind the scenery, it's all fake. But it amazes me how people can sit for hours listening to an actor emote about someone else's problems and fail to recognize their own condition. The stage is a metaphor for the world. For life. For something. *Angrily.* Who are you, anyway? And what's the point of this audition?

VOICE: Your time's up.

QUINN: But I'm just getting started.

VOICE: It says here that your name is Quinn. Is that male or female?

QUINN: *Startled.* What did you say?

VOICE: Are you male or female?

QUINN: What difference does that make? I want to be Romeo *and* Juliet, Othello *and* Desdemona. I want to lead armies into battle, depose kings, and rage against the darkness. *Pauses.* In other words, I am not what I seem. "One face, one voice, one habit, and two persons. Thus play I many people, and none contented." *Glares out front.* That's from Shakespeare, too, in case you don't recognize it.

VOICE: I said your time's up. NEXT!

The pool of bright light disappears. Quinn looks around and then signals to the control booth at the rear of the theatre until the light returns.

QUINN: I have one more thing to say. Now you see me. Now you don't.

He signals again and the whole stage suddenly goes dark.

VOICE: *From the darkness.* Why did you do that, Quinn?

QUINN: Because I wanted to, that's why. *Pauses.* And because the lighting technician is my partner who told me about the audition and dared me to do it.

After a moment of silence, the house lights come up to reveal an empty stage.

The Accidental Universe

History is the version of past events that people have decided to agree upon. —*Napoleon Bonaparte*

I. EXCREMENTAL HISTORY

My name is Americus and I am the voice of history. I mean all history, past and present, not just the names, dates, and places we had to memorize in school. Although I've spent my professional life studying the facts of history, I've also managed to find humor in what I've found. When a statue of Christopher Columbus was recently pulled down in Baltimore and tossed into the harbor, members of the local chapter of the Sons of Italy were not happy. But they would have been even more upset to learn about some of their hero's bizarre beliefs. On his third voyage to America, Columbus came to the conclusion that the earth was not round, but pear shaped.

At the top of this pear was a protrusion which he described as "something like a woman's nipple" and that's where he believed the lost Garden of Eden was located. Needless to say, Columbus never found the nipple or Paradise, at least not in this life.

My favorite religious painting from the Middle Ages shows a monstrous Satan eating and excreting the souls of the damned, an image that leaves little to the imagination. Actually, there's a lot of excretion in human history. Modern psychologists say that our most pleasurable experiences are sex, eating, and shitting, in that order. My first publication was about the Mayans of Central America who built spectacular pyramids to worship their gods, drank blood in their coffee, sacrificed their fellow countrymen to appease the same gods, and played soccer with the decapitated heads of their enemies. They also must have shit a lot, because one reason their civilization died out so quickly is that they paved over their public spaces with impervious stones which prevented the run-off of human waste. There are many other civilizations, like the Mayans, that have totally disappeared from the face of the earth. I explored some of them in my most recent book, which proposes that history is often made up of random incidents that resulted in unintended consequences. My friend Chris jokingly referred to this as my *shit happens* theory, but I prefer to call it excremental history. Another example is the interstellar object which recently passed through our solar system. Some scientists said it came from an alien technology, but based on its color and shape—long, thin, and brown—I think it's a cosmic example of my theory. One late night TV host jokingly referred to it as part of a NASA program called Turds in Space.

There have also been numerous examples of distorted or partial truths throughout history. Most people know that Gutenberg's invention of the printing press resulted in the first translation of the Bible into German, which enabled Martin Luther to publish his Ninety-Five Theses and led to the Protestant revolution. But Luther wrote a lesser known treatise entitled "On the Jews and Their Lies," which encouraged people to destroy the homes, schools, and synagogues of the Jewish population and eventually led to the expulsion of Jews from many European countries. Some may deny this fact, because there are now competing versions of history. Based on my own research, I have concluded that a great deal of history is the result of unpredictable events. Napoleon invaded Russia with half a million troops but left with a mere ten thousand because of that country's freezing temperatures. When unpredictable and tragic things happened in the ancient world, they were attributed to fate or to gods who enjoyed watching us suffer. In the Christian era, it was thought to be God's will that we achieve salvation through suffering. But I believe religion has done more harm than good to humanity.

I didn't always think that way. I was raised a Catholic and grew up in a working-class neighborhood of Washington D.C., not far from some of the historical monuments. I was given the name Americus because my grandfather had emigrated from Italy to America. My mother gave me the more conventional middle name of Guglielmo, which is Italian for William. When I started grade school the nuns weren't too happy with either one, so I went by the name of Will. My father was a Navy man who fell in love with the water. After serving in the military, he became a plumber and bought a small boat, which I helped care for by scrubbing barnacles off the hull during the hot summer months. My mother died when I was three years old, so I was raised by my aunt Judy, who helped care for me until her mind began to fail. By the time I reached high school she couldn't remember any of her friends, the boat trips she took with my dad, or the amusement park we often went to. Then one day she fell asleep and never woke up, as if escaping to some heavenly realm. I expected my father might do the same, but he was an intense smoker and passed quickly from lung cancer when I was in college. He was a man of few words, but as he lay dying in the hospital he wanted to talk about the past, things he remembered that still bothered him in some way. I was embarrassed to hear the secrets of his life but I held his hand until his last breath. Then I reached up and gently closed his eyes. When I recall that moment now, I feel guilty for not telling him I loved him or how grateful I was for all he had done for me.

I was the only kid from our inner city neighborhood to attend Gonzaga, a Jesuit high school not far from the U.S. Capitol. We studied Latin with the goal of understanding it without having to translate, a skill the Jesuits called sight reading. Our teacher said that by senior year we would be able to sight read Virgil's *Aeneid*, which he claimed Shakespeare did in grammar school. We learned about the pre-Socratic philosophers who disagreed over whether the universe was orderly and unchanging or in a state of random and constant flux. I did well in Latin but struggled with ancient Greek, so I had to read most of Plato and Aristotle in translation. I liked what Aristotle said about how it was impossible to appreciate pleasure without having experienced pain, and my favorite passage from Plato was the speech by Socrates just before he drank the hemlock. Gonzaga played football and basketball against another Jesuit school called Georgetown Prep, which was my first contact with the suburban elite of Washington. I soon realized how different they were from us, with their preppy clothes, fancy cars, and snobbish attitude. The Jesuits taught us to question everything with reason or logic, and they were so successful that I eventually questioned the religion they practiced. After graduating from Gonzaga, I won a scholarship to Georgetown University, where I majored in history with a minor in Elizabethan drama that included courses at the Folger Shakespeare Library.

After Georgetown I went to Yale to study for a doctorate in ancient history. While teaching undergraduates there in a lecture hall seating several hundred students, I sometimes posed the question *What is truth?* Most of them were slumped in their seats or pretending to take notes, but whenever I asked that question a few would sit up and stare at me as if I had descended from the clouds. I understand now there are no definitive answers to that question. Sadly, in our contemporary world, truth is whatever you choose to believe. As a result, my life's work will mean nothing to those who are burning the books of history by ignoring the facts.

I met two other graduate students at Yale who quickly became the most important people in my life. Chris came from a strict Evangelical background and was majoring in biblical studies at the School of Divinity but changed his beliefs while at Yale. We often discussed religion or history over beers at a local bar. One night, he brought along a young woman whom he introduced by saying, "You two have a mutual interest in Shakespeare." Julia was earning her doctorate in Shakespeare studies and had a particular interest in the female characters of his plays. She was beautiful and brilliant, determined and decidedly feminist. Most of all, with her sparkling wit and unbounded energy, she was fun to be with. After we started dating, I discovered her gentler, kinder side—and her sincere interest in other people. We read many of Shakespeare's plays together, taking different roles and discussing our interpretations. We ended up living together for most of that year before deciding to get married. As poor graduate students short on both time and money, we decided to have a simple wedding and were thrilled when Chris agreed to perform the ceremony.

Then, blinded by the present, I forgot my painful past. The clearest lesson of history is that we all must die and the last thing my father said as he lay dying was something about the sea. The last thing Julia would say was something about Shakespeare. After finishing her degree, she was awarded a grant to spend the summer doing research in London about the role of women in Shakespeare's plays. Because I had to stay at Yale to work on my doctoral thesis, we agreed to meet in Italy for a short vacation after she finished her research. By then she had made an important discovery and said she couldn't wait to share it with me. We met in Rome in August and were crossing a busy street in front of the train station when she forgot that she wasn't in England. She looked right instead of left, then stepped off the curb and was hit by a passing car. I can still hear the deadly thud that marked the end of her life, a tragedy from which I will never recover.

I managed to finish my thesis the following year and was looking for a further distraction from grief when Chris invited me to join him on a research project in the Middle East. He said he needed someone with extensive knowledge of ancient history and languages. That experience in the Holy Land would eventually result in a book in which I showed how religion has been the cause of suffering, ignorance, and intolerance throughout history. I cited the persecution of Jews by Catholics in the Middle Ages, of Catholics by Protestants after the Reformation, and between Muslims and Christians throughout history. Needless to say, I was attacked by zealous defenders of many religious sects as a result. Shortly after I returned from the Holy Land, I visited a distant cousin of my father's in Baltimore on his 95th birthday. When I asked Sam Marinelli how he managed to survive for so long, he responded with a shrug and a smile. "Life is a crap shoot," he said. He summed up in five simple words what I would spend decades trying to prove. I proposed in my next book that all of human history is random, meaningless, and subjective, a conclusion which coincides with my personal feelings about the world and our place in it. I wanted to call it *The Excremental Theory of History*, but my editor laughed and said the publisher would never agree to that. We settled instead on *The Accidental Universe.*

II. HEAVENLY MUSIC

My name is Christian and I am the voice of heaven. At least I used to be. I'm the only son of born-again fundamentalists who gave me that name. I was home schooled and learned at an early age that everything in the Bible is the inspired word of God. Also that the earth is only six thousand years old. Ironically, I never questioned these so-called facts until I went to college and majored in biblical studies. That's when I began to wonder why the God of the Old Testament was often angry and vengeful. But it was only after I went to the Yale School of Divinity for graduate work that I learned about the many significant problems with biblical texts. For example, there are over 5,000 surviving manuscripts of the New Testament and no two are exactly alike. Likewise, an early text of the Old Testament says that a young girl would conceive and bring forth a son, but the term *young girl* was translated by the evangelists into the Greek word for virgin. As a result, the Roman Catholic Church concluded that Mary was a perpetual virgin before, during, and after the birth of Jesus.

I'm now an agnostic anti-biblical scholar but I still believe that many stories from the Old Testament have a message for our contemporary world. The Book of Genesis says "The earth was without form and void, and darkness was upon the deep." That sounds like an image from the Hubble telescope and raises the question *What and where is heaven?* Unlike Michelangelo, we know that beyond all those beautiful billowing clouds and glorious sunsets there is only darkness and the cold abyss of space. Perhaps the most famous story from the Book of Genesis is about Adam and Eve. Years ago, while on a trip to Rome, I saw a sculpture depicting their temptation in the Garden of Eden. The serpent had the head of a woman identical to the head of Eve as she offered the apple to Adam. At that moment I understood for the first time the real meaning of the story. The devil *became* human, which suggests that we are the source of good and evil on earth. God and the devil aren't some remote mythical figures battling it out on a mountaintop. If they exist at all, they're right here, in our heads, in our minds.

My first book, written while I was still at Yale, was a secular history of Jesus in which I showed that he was just one of many messiahs at the time who claimed to be the king of the Jews. His followers were so horrified when he was crucified that most of them ran away. Although the gospel says the soldiers tired of waiting for Jesus to die and pierced his side with a sword, it's unlikely that he was taken down from the cross as depicted in many religious paintings. Crucified bodies were left hanging for days to be eaten by birds of prey as a reminder of the Roman punishment for insurrection. Likewise the gnostic gospels contain very different interpretations of what Jesus said and did. For example, the Gospel of Mary gives us a unique and provocative version of the relationship between Jesus and Mary Magdalene. *Noli me tangere.* That's what the risen Christ said to her. *Don't touch me.* You have to wonder why he would say that when he told the doubting apostle Thomas to put a hand into the open wound of his side. It's clearly another example of contradictory texts. And while the New Testament says that Jesus died a shameful death on the cross, the early bishops of the church concluded that his mother Mary didn't die a natural death. Because she was the mother of God, she was exempt from the physical decay of death brought about by Adam and Eve, and was assumed bodily into heaven.

In my second book, I explained that neither heaven nor hell is specifically mentioned in the Old Testament. No trumpets sounding and no heavenly host of angelic choirs singing. These are the invention of medieval monks who wrote to please their superiors by creating visions that would inspire or motivate the faithful. Gregorian chant and the soaring melodies of Hildegard von Bingen are the closest things to heavenly music we will ever hear. My best friend from Yale feels the same way. A historian who is skeptical about the influence of religion on history, he goes by the name of Will even though his first name is Americus. He's still grieving over the recent death of his wife who was also a dear friend of mine, so I've invited him to join me on a field trip to the Holy Land where I plan to do research on the origin of the gnostic gospels. The area we'll be working in is still considered dangerous because of unexploded bombs from the 1967 war between Israel and Syria. When I mentioned this to Will, he laughed and said, "How ironic would it be for two former Christians to die together in the Holy Land?"

III. WHAT YOU WILL

My name is Julia and I am the voice of Shakespeare. Not that cad, William, but his poor wife Anne. A lot has been written about her lately, but I'm curious why she's always referred to as Anne Hathaway rather than by her married name. Her famous husband left her with four children while he ran off to London to perform on the stage, and she had to bury their son Hamnet when he died at the age of eleven from the plague. Then, to add insult to injury, her husband bequeathed her their "second best bed" in his will with no mention of books, manuscripts, or his shares in a successful London theatre company. How did he expect her to survive? Of course that question has plagued many women for centuries, and one more example won't rewrite history. My doctoral thesis at Yale was entitled *The Women of Shakespeare* and it describes how most of his female characters were not typical women of the time. They had important roles in many of his plays and sometimes significantly altered the plot.

After completing my doctorate, I received a grant to research the topic further in a private London library where I made an incredible discovery. As a result, I can now prove conclusively who is the real author of Shakespeare's works. I had already begun to question some of the assumptions about his early life even before I began the program at Yale. Not the brilliance of his works, but what seemed to me preconceived notions about who he was and what we know from the time of his childhood. The plays and sonnets of Shakespeare are without a doubt among the greatest works ever written in the English language, yet even the most knowledgeable experts of his dramaturgy continue to gloss over significant gaps in what we know about his life. Many authors who defend the authorship of Shakespeare have spent their entire careers writing about him, so the reputation and livelihood of these mostly male scholars depends on the ongoing fiction about the man from Stratford. They invariably use phrases like *would have*, *could have*, and *most likely* to explain how he acquired his knowledge of history and foreign countries as well as the behavior of nobility at the court of Queen Elizabeth. They are fond of citing how much we know about the performance and publication of plays in the sixteenth century but fail to mention how little we actually know about the actor named William Shakespeare. In any other scholarly field such dodging of the truth would be unheard of.

When I learned in graduate school that Shakespeare contributed nearly two thousand words to the English language, I wondered how a glove maker's son with only a grammar school education could have done so. There are actually two key questions about the controversy of his authorship. Could a poorly educated man from a small rural town in sixteenth century England write such incredible works and, if he didn't, who did? My summer grant to conduct research in the private library of William Cecil, Lord Chancellor to Queen Elizabeth, provided an unexpected answer to both questions. While there I came across a play about a sixteenth century theatre troupe that often disagreed about what new works to present. My chance discovery of the play entitled "What You Will" confirmed my suspicions that William Shakespeare was not the true author of the works attributed to him. It contained a play within the play about the real author of the company's most popular productions, who was a member of the nobility and a patron who arranged for the troupe to perform his works at court. "What You Will" was hidden among a collection of works donated by the Earl of Oxford to the family of his father-in-law, William Cecil. On his deathbed the Earl dedicated the new play to an actor who had helped him work out the staging of his earlier works. The dedication reads as follows. "To my friend Will, who hath led me gently but firmly to that undiscovered country wherein I have happily resided for lo these many years." This clearly implied that the real author of Shakespeare's plays was none other than Edward de Vere, the Earl of Oxford.

There are also numerous internal or textual reasons for questioning the authorship of Shakespeare's plays, including my favorite quote from "Hamlet." *There is nothing either good or bad but thinking makes it so.* With these words the Prince of Denmark suggests that all truth is relative, an incredibly modern statement for anyone to make in the sixteenth century. Whoever penned those words was far ahead of his time and far above the level of education he would have received in a small country town like Stratford. Hamlet says that his own education was in Wittenberg, Germany, where Martin Luther lived and wrote. This implies that the author of "Hamlet" also knew about Luther's claim that anyone can interpret the Bible as they see fit, a proposition which led to the Protestant Revolution. Such an incredible insight must have been written by a highly educated person of the Elizabethan nobility such as Edward de Vere.

Despite the unmistakable implications of "What You Will,"

there are those who will continue to deny the true identity of the author. In today's world people decide what to believe based on their own background and experience rather than on hard evidence or facts. Ironically that's exactly the meaning of the speech by Hamlet I just referred to. Finding a play entitled "What You Will" was not only random and unexpected, but also ironic because it's the sub-title of Shakespeare's comedy "Twelfth Night" in which role reversal and other examples of disorder or mayhem abound. And if we live in a world where truth is relative, as Hamlet suggested, then the question of who wrote the plays attributed to Shakespeare doesn't matter as much as the beauty and brilliance they contain.

The challenge for me now is to publish my conclusions based on the discovery of "What You Will." My work may not be accepted because I am young and female and not yet well known in the field of Shakespeare studies. I'm counting on my husband---whose name is also Will, and has published scholarly works in the field of history---to offer suggestions on how to submit my findings. Once I have completed my research in London, we plan to meet for a brief holiday in Italy and visit Verona, the city where "Romeo and Juliet" takes place.

IV. TRUE ENOUGH

Chris warned me of the danger before we began our search of ruins on the West Bank that might yield information vital to interpreting the gnostic gospels. He said the area still contained active land mines from the 1967 war, when the so-called Holy Land became what he called the Land of Holy War. After several months working in unbearable heat and dust at the first site, we headed for our second destination. On the way, Chris decided to stop by the side of the road to check his bearings. He walked with his map a short distance away from the jeep and gazed at a distant mountain before turning back. I knew what happened as soon as I heard the muffled explosion and saw the cloud of smoke. He was gone in an instant, just like Julia. I have often replayed both scenes in my mind and asked myself *Why? Why them and not me?* But if history is random and unpredictable, then why should our own lives be any different? Chris disproved the accepted truths about Jesus, even though that was not his original intent in studying the Bible. And Julia was able to question the authorship of Shakespeare's works after accidentally stumbling on a play by the Earl of Oxford.

After Julia's death I tried repeatedly to have her work published, but the play was never authenticated to the satisfaction of Shakespeare scholars, and the private library where it was found eventually refused further access. By then, the future of my career as a respected historian was questionable because of my random theory of history. Fortunately, I found a small university in the Mid-West that offered me a tenure track position and spent the next thirty years there teaching Humanities, a subject that combined my love of history, languages, literature, and the arts. My students were not happy when I announced on the first day of class that nobody would get an A, only a few would get B's or C's, and the rest would get D's or F's. My purpose was to make them work harder, and it usually succeeded. On my teacher evaluations some students said I was very knowledgeable and cared passionately about what I taught. Others said I was arrogant, condescending, pompous, and anal. I especially liked that last adjective. Their comments are preserved forever on a website called *Rate Your Professor*. After my retirement I learned that I was also known as "Professor G" because I considered myself a god in the classroom. I knew it was time to retire when the curriculum was updated to include such topics as Humanities of the Self, Humanities of the Body, Animal Humanities, and the inevitable Digital Humanities.

But then, in an ironic twist of fate, something remarkable happened. My theories about the randomness of history and the subjective meaning of truth were verified by hard science. A Nobel Prize winning biologist named Jacques Monod proved that some genetic mutations of the human DNA code are in fact random occurrences. In an instant molecular biology upended all philosophical and religious claims of our origin or purpose. Likewise, physicists soon concluded that deadly deposits of iridium on earth were the result of an errant asteroid accidently striking our planet around the same time that dinosaurs became extinct. And robotic telescopes detected what is called dark energy, confirming the theory that the universe is still expanding. As a result, some of the world's leading physicists have proposed that our universe is only one of many possible universes and their existence came about by accident. These discoveries offer conclusive evidence that the evolution of our physical environment is the result of chance and the same is true for human life. I was right after all. So were Chris and Julia. If we live in an accidental universe, then the bible is not the inspired word of an intentional god, the Earl of Oxford could very well be the real author of Shakespeare's works, and truth is indeed relative. I could now expand my *shit happens* theory of history to include the whole cosmos, but no one would pay attention, let alone believe me.

Lately, I feel overwhelmed by the relentless passing of time as my mind moves back and forth between past and present like sand flowing through an hourglass. Sometimes I walk in my sleep among the dead in a scene of battle or plague like some Medieval painting. Or I wake up in the middle of the night full of vivid memories. My aunt Judy falling asleep to escape this life. My father on his deathbed as he struggled to breathe. The terrible sound of Julia being struck by a car and the sight of Chris disappearing in a cloud of smoke. Such images have persisted for decades and I can't wipe them from my consciousness. I know these people I cared for would be different now if they were alive, but I prefer to remember them as they once were because I still miss them very much.

Now, as Shakespeare would say, the times are out of joint. As I write this, a great pandemic is spreading across the globe and the world is in chaos as never before. Many thousands have already died, with millions more likely to come. Despite what some religious leaders may proclaim, it's neither a divine punishment nor a sign of the Rapture but simply history repeating itself. The Black Death wiped out a third of Europe in the 14th century, surfaced again in the 16th century shortly after the birth of Shakespeare, and ravaged England throughout his lifetime. He rarely mentioned it in his works, but when he did there is no mistaking what it must have been like, with "sighs and groans and shrieks that rend the air." In the midst of the pandemic, I remind myself that more than a hundred billion people have lived since the beginning of human history, each one a unique consciousness. There are more neurons in a single human brain than there are planets in our galaxy. I believe that our brain is like the accidental universe, mysterious and unpredictable, and because each mind is its own universe, there will always be multiple interpretations of the truth. Which leads to the ultimate question: *How can we find meaning in an accidental universe bookended by nothingness?*

Everything I've told you here is true. Every fact, every quote, every reference and example. Only the personal stories have been altered. So we come at last to the end, to the only question that matters and the one that now preoccupies me the most. *How do I face death, the most universal and feared of human experiences?* I know what death is like because I've watched it happen, held hands with it, and dreamt about it. Instead of chafing against fate or resisting the flow of time, I prefer to believe what Socrates said just before he died. Death may be the greatest of all human blessings, either a state of nothingness and utter unconsciousness, or else a migration of the soul from this world to another where we will encounter those we knew and loved. Whatever or wherever it is, I will be happy to sleep peacefully in that place. Unlike what happened to those who were dearest to me, my own demise is predictable. Because death is imminent with no expectation of recovery, I have directed that my life not be extended by artificial means. I especially forbid uploading the content of my brain to a computer. That's not the kind of immortality I want. I prefer a peaceful end when past and present become one in a single moment of awareness and release. I can sense that happening now.

I have become history.

A.G. "Will" Rizzo

Discussion Questions

Which stories mention real historical figures or events?

What well known artists or writers are the subjects of a story?

What line from Hamlet can be found in the play "Hole in the Ground"?

Who are the three historical characters in the play "Waiting for Will"?

What famous American artist supposedly coined the phrase *fifteen minutes of fame*?

What modern playwright described the human condition as Janus does with the words "They give birth astride of a grave"?

Most of the stories are set in a specific time and place. Are any set outside of time?

What is meant by the term accidental universe? What specific examples of this are found in the stories?

What other themes, ideas, or questions are raised?

About the Author

A native of Baltimore, Gerard Marconi earned a master's degree in Humanities from Johns Hopkins University and in Theatre from Catholic University. He taught these subjects and held related administrative positions at the college level for many years. As Coordinator of Cultural Affairs at the Rose Lehrman Arts Center in Harrisburg, Pennsylvania, he initiated a lecture series that brought to the community college campus such well known speakers as John Barth, Nora Ephron, and Maya Angelou. He led study tours to museums and theaters in Baltimore, Washington, London, and Florence, Italy, and served on the boards of the Theatre Association of Pennsylvania, the Dance Council of Central Pennsylvania, and the Frederick Arts Council in Maryland. He studied fiction writing in classes or seminars with Lee K. Abbott, Roxanne Robinson, Alexander Chee, and Jennifer Haigh. His short stories have appeared in *The Chattahoochee Review*, *Somerset Review*, *The Write Launch*, and *Mayday Magazine*, among others, and his one-act play entitled "Rapture" was given a public reading by the Baltimore Playwrights Festival.

Apprentice
House Press
Loyola University Maryland

Apprentice House is the country's only campus-based, student-staffed book publishing company. Directed by professors and industry professionals, it is a nonprofit activity of the Communication Department at Loyola University Maryland.

Using state-of-the-art technology and an experiential learning model of education, Apprentice House publishes books in untraditional ways. This dual responsibility as publishers and educators creates an unprecedented collaborative environment among faculty and students, while teaching tomorrow's editors, designers, and marketers.

Eclectic and provocative, Apprentice House titles intend to entertain as well as spark dialogue on a variety of topics. Financial contributions to sustain the press's work are welcomed. Contributions are tax deductible to the fullest extent allowed by the IRS.

To learn more about Apprentice House books or to obtain submission guidelines, please visit www.apprenticehouse.com.

Apprentice House
Communication Department
Loyola University Maryland
4501 N. Charles Street
Baltimore, MD 21210
410-617-5265
info@apprenticehouse.com
www.apprenticehouse.com